EVOLUTIONARY

AGENTS

TIMOTHY LEARY

Translated by Beverly A. Potter, Ph.D.

RONIN
Berkeley, CA

EVOLUTIONARY AGENTS

ISBN: 1-57951-064-7

Published by
RONIN Publishing, Inc.
PO Box 22900
Oakland, CA 94609
www.roninpub.com

Credits:

Translater:	**Beverly A. Potter, Ph.D.** www.docpotter.com
Editor:	**Barry Katzmann** katzmann@comedyday.com
Cover art:	**David Cabot** CabotArt@cs.com
Cover design:	**Beverly A. Potter**
Text font:	Venus by Chank www.chank.com
Cover fonts:	Sodom by Chank
	Venus by Chank

Distributed to the trade by **Publishers Group West**
Printed in the United States of America by United Graphics
Library of Congress Card Number — 2004095347
Printing Number 1

Derived from *The Intelligence Agents,* by Beverly A. Potter, Ph.D.

RONIN BOOKS BY TIMOTHY LEARY

BEHIND YOUR FOREHEAD YOU CARRY AROUND A 100 BILLION-CELL BIOELECTRIC COMPUTER THAT CREATES REALITIES.

TABLE OF CONTENTS

THE
SMART
THING
TO DO
IS TO
GET
SMARTER.

EVOLVE
OR DIE!

1

WHAT'S AN EVOLUTIONARY AGENT?

EVOLUTIONARY AGENTS CHART THE PATH to the future. They prefabricate future visions, build new hives, custom make plan-its, encourage migration, and teach scientific mastery of the nervous system as an instrument to decode atomic, molecular and subnuclear processes so as to attain immortality, cloning, and extraterrestrial existence.

ROOTS

EVOLUTIONARY AGENTS STUDY HISTORY because understanding our roots is important. We can't navigate into the future with any confidence unless we understand the rhythms and coherence of past voyages. A philosopher demonstrates understanding of the past by the accuracy of predictions about the future. After we trace our roots backward—back East—*it's necessary* **WATCH OUT!** *to move westward into The Future.*

The time has come to catch the coming waves rolling into the future. They're going to be big ones.

In this book, we'll survey the creation of the future, the evolution of intelligence and the three great change processes employed by deoxyribonucleic acid (DNA).

DNA CHANGE PROCESSES

Mutation—A species getting smarter.

Metamorphosis—Individuals getting smarter.

Migration—Individuals moving to a new space to better live out new capacities.

Every time you improve, every time you change, every time a challenge increases your intelligence, you have to migrate to find a new space to live out your new capacity, to custom-make your new vision. Mobility is the classic stimulus for Intelligence Increase, I^2. Learn to be comfortable with the idea of change.

Understanding how our intelligence has evolved reveals who we are. The strategy of evolution is to raise the intelligence of species. Don't let others scare you about change. We each pass through at least twelve volatile and dramatic changes during our life times. Each of us possesses within our nervous systems twelve primitive brains that emerge in sequence as we develop—evolve if you will—from infancy to adult maturity. Cryptographic decoding of the DNA helix suggests that each of us has twelve post-terrestrial brains scheduled to activate in sequence as we move into and prefabricate the post-hive future!

LEARN TO BE COMFORTABLE WITH THE IDEA OF CHANGE.

OUT-CASTES

TERRESTRIAL THEOLOGIANS RECOGNIZE THE SUPERNATURAL and otherworldly powers of great Evolutionary Agents like Buddha, Christ, and Krishna that separate them in time and potency from the hive reality. "Supernatural" is jargon to describe anything beyond hive-platitude.

Often Evolutionary Agents must endure long periods of quiescence and obscurity. These can be times of grave peril, obstruction or hive-disgrace. Evolutionary Agents, also known as *Out-Castes,* have been selected on the basis of their capacity to face and survive experiences that would be judged unendurable by terrestrials. Agents' childhoods abound in anecdotes of precocious sagacity, strength, and independence from hive-mortals. The scandalous escapades of Krishna, the prowess of Hercules, the boyish wisdom of Einstein, the early verbal cleverness of the Galileo, and the patience of Robert Goddard are a few examples.

Human beings, pre-selected from each gene pool, are having their neural circuits activated—usually without their awareness—to fabricate future realities as well as future gene pools. These individuals are genetically templated to live much of the time in the future. They are, to a large extent, alienated from current hive realities. Unaware of their genetic assignment, many Agents feel agonizingly out of step. Some are shunned and even locked up by the gene pools they serve.

EVOLUTIONARY AGENTS MAY ENDURE LONG PERIODS OF QUIESCENCE, OBSCURITY AND EVEN HIVE-DISGRACE.

Those who are lucky enough to recognize their post-human genetic caste attain a level of great prescience and humorous insight. They understand

MANY AGENTS FEEL AGONIZINGLY OUT OF STEP.

that they are time travelers, literally walking around in past civilizations—a most entertaining and effective role to play. While they have little power to change the ripples of history or the waves of evolution, they surf them with increasing skill.

As out-castes they are cast out, thrown forward, pushed up, above and beyond, contemporary hive realities.

Such Evolutionary Agents are best described as Out-Castes. They are cast out, thrown forward, pushed up, above and beyond, contemporary hive realities. As evolution accelerates increasing numbers of Evolutionary Agents are emerging. In the 1960s every gene pool cast out its Futique Agents. We are now learning to identify these out-castes and how to benefit from their contribution to the species.

AGENT CASTE

THE WORD "AGENT" HAS BEEN IN WELL-DESERVED ILL-REPUTE, especially in political, diplomatic and showbiz circles. It suggests an unscrupulous bureaucratic scoundrel devoid of creativity, aesthetics, principles or talent who, by virtue of shameless cunning, places himself in central positions of power and control.

The raison d'être of the agent is, of course, the deal. The deal involves the alchemy of link-up, package and connection. The agent's tools are persuasion, negotiation, bluff, manipulation, and salesmanship.

The Agent Caste has existed throughout human history, dating back to the Neolithic period when artifacts, abstract-concepts, symbols, intertribal barter systems, and paperwork began to replace direct face-to-face interactions within tribe exchanges. As left-hemisphere technological society emerged, each gene pool produced Agents to represent the assets and interests of the sperm-egg collective in dealing with other gene-colonies.

In Feudal times, agents represented the Crown or the Lord in dealing with serfs, peasants, tenants, traders and the agents of other Lords. The sordid odor attributed to agents probably dates back to their role as ruthless tax-collectors, dishonest traders, not to forget the many incidents in which agents betrayed their masters to seize power.

The Caste of Agents took on more importance and a more attractive appearance during the emergence of democratic societies when agents became political representatives of the various classes, castes, guilds, brotherhoods, and gene pools which sought to share power in a democratic tradition.

AGENTS CONTROL, THE DEAL.

The history of civilization is the history of agentry, which is to be

THE HISTORY OF CIVILIZATION IS THE HISTORY OF AGENTRY.

expected since agents cunningly arrange for the publication of the history books. Wars are won and lost by generals, but when the smoke clears and the bodies are dragged off the battlefield, the real bottom-line stuff happens—the peace treaties, the Councils of Nice, Trent, Versailles, Vienna, Geneva—all managed by agents. When the autobiographies are written and generals from both sides peddle their memoirs, it is the agents who make the deals.

The high-points in the annals of agentry have always come at moments of species mutation. Who has not marveled at the astuteness of Algy Plancton, the re-nowned Paleozoic agent who put together the first oxygen commercials which led to shoreline migration?

REALITY MOVIE MAKERS

RON BERNSTEIN WELL-DESERVES HIS PLACE in the Agents Hall of Fame. After a brilliant career as a movie producer and literary manager, Bernstein started what is known as the "Bernstein Age of Show-Business." The key to his success was synergy—the assemblage of many elements in a blockbuster molecule of enormous complexity. This technique was developed in its primitive form by the Australian migrant, Robert Stigwood, who used the one-hundred-million dollar

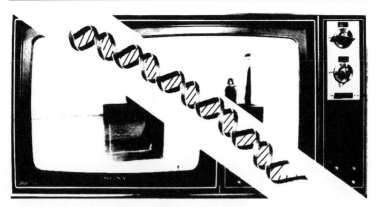

movie *Saturday Night Fever* as little more than a record album commercial.

George Lucas, another synergy pioneer, used the half-billion-dollar movie, *Star Wars,* as an advertising trailer for his souvenir marketing business. Henry Edwards, another early media-alchemist, used a 110-million-dollar movie and a 150-million dollar album as promotion for his Pulitzer Prize winning novel *Sgt. Pepper's Lonely Hearts Club Band.*

Legend has it that Ron Bernstein, upon observing how movies, TV shows, albums, novelizations were used as hype for each other, came to the startling conclusion that totally changed human ontology. "Why not use all forms of media, working together synergistically, to hype future reality?"

Bernstein thus became the first Reality Movie Maker. If movies could get people to buy albums—why then movies could get people to buy realities. After all, movies are reality simulations. This is how reality became a spin-off of showbiz. And, **MOVIES GET PEOPLE TO BUY REALITIES.** indeed, "Reality TV" burst forth in popularity as we crossed the cusp into the 21st Century.

2

NEUROGENICS

OUR KNOWLEDGE OF HUMAN NEUROGENETICS is so primitive that we've only recently realized that structural and temporal castes exist. Sociobiologists and ethologists define their professions as the study of behavioral genetics. However, neurogenetics is a more accurate description because what is inherited is not behavior but neural templates that determine use of the anatomical-technology.

What is inherited is not behavior but neural templates

Local hive behavior cues—language, customs, artifacts, and the like are not genetically inherited—they are cultural imprints. Only the caste-circuits are inherited, not the behaviors, which are acquired in a cultural context. Until ethologists understand the difference between neurogenetic castes and local-social-imprints, their brilliant observations cannot be mapped.

LOCAL HIVE BEHAVIOR CUES ARE CULTURAL IMPRINTS.

This insight is changing our conceptions of human nature and society. It is probable that we are neurologically programmed so that understanding of castes becomes part of *species contelligence*—consciousness + intelligence—only at the time that space migration occurs. Plan-It Colonies in High Orbit provide the new ecological vacuum in which human caste differences can blossom without the friction and crowded competition that has colored Earthly racial-class-sexual-caste differences.

You must realize that we are a genetic-caste-robot to understand your own personal development. John Lilly articulates this beautifully in *Programming the Human BioComputer.* We are templated by DNA to play a certain role. We are outfitted with a 24-gear brain that is very different from 92% of other human brains.

TWELVE SURVIVAL TACTICS

THE VENERABLE LANGUAGE OF ZODIAC TYPES IS USEFUL to start a dialogue about casting. The twelve signs of the Zodiac are useful labels for basic structural human castes. Philosophers—good ones—are human ethologists. For five thousand years, the most shrewd human ethologists have worked on this twelve-fold typecasting—based on extensive and empirical observation. If we ignore the "astro" part we are left with the "logic" of twelve survival tactics—Pisces, Aries, etc. In the future more sophisticated classifications of human types based on neurological differences will replace the crude zodiac classification.

PHILOSOPHERS ARE HUMAN ETHOLOGISTS.

There will be some among you, those of scientific and intellectual bent, who are offended by use of this "sloppy occult astrological superstitious" technology. Before you fuse out, reread the crude, generalized list of the twelve personality types. Admittedly, astrology is a primitive attempt at introducing the notion of temporal caste, seriality and developmental order. The survival characteristic assigned to each type describes an evolutionary technology and a developmental stage. Pisces is baby and amoeboid. Aquarius is the most elderly, orderly, mature. Sense how this list tries to recapitulate the evolution of the twelve basic neurotechnological functions—both in the species and individuals. We can reject this list when we can replace it by a better personality typology based on the sequential evolution of intelligence, in species and in individuals. For now, however, it is a useful system.

Intellectuals, scholars, academics, salaried scientists and all other categories of verbal bureaucrats unanimously denounce astrology. Such condemnation immediately alerts Evolutionary Agents that an important genetic nerve is being touched. These paper-pedants and their civil-service followers make such solemn, judicial pronouncements as: "I don't believe in astrology." This statement means: "I don't understand seasonal ethology and I automatically reject everything my brain is not wired to receive."

Look, therefore, for the valid reasons why hive philosophers fear astrology and you will find, hidden in the tangle of zodiac ravings, three important items of neurogenetic wisdom.

WISDOM OF THE ZODIAC

1) Regular cycles influence neural development.

2) Each of us is born a robot, templated and controlled by rhythms with which we can decipher and harmonize.

3) Each of us is born into a caste, or into a complex of castes.

Suspend belief and assume, for the moment, that Zodiac types define structural castes. Each of the twelve terrestrial intelligence-functions plays an important role in the human social molecule. No human gene pool can exist unless it has people and institutions playing out these twelve neurotechnological parts.

Each of the twelve terrestrial intelligence-functions plays an important role in the human social molecule.

TEMPORAL CASTE

IT IS THE GENIUS—GENETIC-VOLATILITY—OF HUMANITY that, although each of us is a genetic-robot, we pass through twelve stages as we mature. What a wondrous package, indeed is WoMan! Each of us represents one of the twelve intelligence-survival-solutions and each of us, in maturing, passes through and relives all twelve solutions.

Genetic consciousness allows us to discard old outmoded hive-reality maps, to file away and retire, every previous theological and philosophic blue-print—except those which are based on continual evolution. This does not mean that you should reject empirical data or close-off information or ignore opinions. Be open to every stupidity, savagery, rigidity of the Newtonian natives. Listen to the Christian Fundamentalists when they shout that the *Bible* is a word-for-word revelation and you gain insight into the parroting, Paleolithic, humanoid brain.

Note everything that the primitives say. Then check your own behavior for
   parrot-brained rote repetition.

Study and then file-away orthodox Darwinian blind-selection theories, while respecting the field reports of evolutionists and ethologists. Play with the notions of structural and temporal caste as they affect you. Admire this clever twelve tactic process that allows each of us to recapitulate evolution and to move ahead to create The Future.

ALPHA REALITY

For now let us assume that your genetic template determines your structural caste which, in turn, determines your lifelong *reality attitude*. Attitude is used in the high-altitude, high-velocity aeronautical context—angle of approach. Your structural caste is your *Alpha Reality.*

ATTITUDE IS YOUR ANGLE OF APPROACH.

Find your robot-structural-caste—your DNA Alpha Reality—in the left-column of the Table below and then slide along the twelve developmental stages—CNS Beta Realities—through which you have passed. How can we fail to exult in this blueprint that enables us to experience—and retrieve from genetic memory—every reality that our evolutionary fore-bearers have offered us?

DNA STRUCTURAL CASTES
THE TWELVE ALPHA REALITY ATTITUDES

Sign	Alpha Reality	Attitude
Pisces	Incorporating Caste	Floating, dreamy, liquid, sucking amoeboid.
Aries	Twisting-Biting Caste	Incisive shark attitude
Taurus	Amphibian Caste	Slow, steady, earthy, crawling shoreline.
Gemini	Quicksilver Caste	Evasive, tricky, rodent.
Cancer	Territorial Caste	Controlling, strong, possessive, mammalian.
Leo	Monkey Caste	Exhibitionistic, active, political.
Virgo	Parrot Caste	Mimicing, fussy, symbol-discriminating, Paleolithic.
Libra	Analytical Caste	Figure-it-out, inventive, orderly Neolithic.
Scorpio	Construction Caste	Engineering, administrative, dealing, architectural

Sagittarius Romantic Caste	Intense, adolescent barbarian.
Capricorn Parental Caste	Domestic, familial, responsible, moralistic.
Aquarius Religious Caste	Conservative, aging, past-oriented.

NEUROLOGICAL DEVELOPMENTAL STAGES

STAGE 1: NEWBORN—AMOEBOID BRAINED

AT THIS STAGE WE OPERATE WITH AMOEBOID BRAINS. At this stage we find newly born babies, the terminally ill, and those with genetic defects.

STAGE 2: INFANT—FISH-BRAINED MENTALITY

AT THIS STAGE WE OPERATE WITH FISH BRAINS, unable to handle gravity. Here we find babies between three months and six months, the bedridden sick, and, again, those with genetic defects.

STAGE 3: CRAWLING BABY—LIZARD-BRAINED

AT THIS STAGE WE FUNCTION AT THE AMPHIBIAN LEVEL of neuroreality. This includes crawling babies, wheelchair invalids, seniles, and people with genetic defects. An enormous percentage of the Gross National Energy (GNE) is devoted to the care of human beings operating at the amoeboid marine or amphibian levels of neural development.

STAGE 4: TODDLERS—RODENT-BRAINED

AT THIS STAGE WE OPERATE at the cunning-rodent-evasive animal level of neural development. This stage includes toddling children and those cunning adults who may be performing civilized tasks, but whose brain-space is rodent-like, along with those who will automatically steal anything they get their paws on and have no concept of social-morality.

STAGE 5: DEMANDING KIDS—MAMMAL-BRAINED

AT THIS STAGE WE OPERATE at the aggressive-mammalian level of neural development—includes children between ages three to five, possessive seniles, and many well-functioning adults who operate like fierce carnivores or Mafia capos—extorting, threatening, controlling turf by coercion.

STAGE 6: TERRITORIAL CHILD—MONKEY-BRAINED

AT THIS STAGE WE OPERATE AT THE MONKEY LEVEL of neural development. This stage includes children ages four to seven, seniles, and millions of adults who may appear to be performing civilized functions, but whose realities are those of exhibitionist primates.

STAGE 7: MIMICKING YOUTH—PARROT-BRAINED

THOSE AT THIS STAGE OPERATE at the Paleolithic level, who are capable of parroting-mimicking neural behavior and nothing more. This group includes children ages five to eight, rote-response seniles, and the millions of well-bodied adults who live at the hunter-gatherer level of existence and survive by performing violent-muscular acts—either criminal, police, military or athletic. Or who, via welfare, are modern gatherers. These innocents are incapable of inventive or independent thought and can only rote-repeat what they are taught.

STAGE 8: RULE-MAKING JUVENILES—CONFORMITY-BRAINED

THOSE AT THIS STAGE OPERATE AT THE NEOLITHIC LEVEL of neural development. This group includes children ages seven to nine, seniles, and those who perform craft-work at the level of simple agriculture, small shop-keeping, and who inhabit ethnic, tribal social realities.

STAGE 9: PRE-ADOLESCENTS—GROUP-BRAINED

AROUND 20 MILLION AMERICANS operate at the caste-priest level of neurogenetic evolution. This group includes preadolescent children ages nine to 12, as well as those who live in ethnic groups directed by priests and where economic division of labor is inherited.

STAGE 10: BARBARIAN TEENAGERS

THOSE AT THIS STAGE OPERATE at the semi-civilized, barbarian, feudal level of reality. This group includes adolescents between the ages of 13 and 20, plus ethnic groups who follow a peasant feudal ethnic-Old-World-religious persuasion.

STAGE 11: DOMESTICATED COMPLIANT ADULTS

AT THIS STAGE WE OPERATE at parental-domestic-protestant-ethic level of historical development. This group includes those between the ages of 20 and 45 who live in a homeowner middle-class free-enterprise reality.

STAGE 12: RETIRING ELDERS

THOSE WHO OPERATE AT THIS LEVEL depend upon a centralized-social-security Demo-poll state. This group includes non-seniles over the age of 45, and those who are neurologically most comfortable in an egalitarian, medicare, uniform-unified-law-and-order ecological niche. Also, those who love the comfort of the politically conservative hive and wish to save its macho-pop culture for the few years remaining before their death.

STAGE 13: ME-GENERATION GROWN-UPS

AT THIS STAGE OF DEVELOPMENT we live in a dom-species post-hive, post-political reality of self-consumerism. This group includes all those who define reality in terms of their own hedonic pleasure and organize their existence in terms of leisure, travel, recreation. This group includes a majority of the 35 million marijuana smokers, the *Playboy* readers, the sexual freedom cultists, and jetsetters.

STAGE 14: SELF-ACTUALIZED ADULTS

THOSE AT THIS STAGE WE LIVE AT THE LEVEL of self-actualization. This group includes liberated graduates of yoga, holistic medicine, sufism and self-actualization programs. Being post-parental, these people make the best parents. They make contelligent decisions about when and how and with whom to breed. They treat their children as mutant arrivals—aliens and friends. They avoid imprinting robot-hive culture and train their children to become self-actualized and self-responsible at the earliest ages.

STAGE 15: HEDONIC NETWORKERS

THOSE AT THIS STAGE LIVE AT THE NEURAL LEVEL of post-social communes, including the Space Plan-It Adepts.

STAGE 16, 17, 18: BRAIN-ACCELERATED ADULTS

AT THESE STAGES OUR BRAINS OPERATE at the Neuroelectric level and we understand the neural-fabrication nature of reality. At this stage we're classified as — Brain-Reality Consumers, Brain Reality Self- Actualizers and Brain-Reality Fusers. These include those who have experienced LSD, plus those geniuses and psychotics who are trapped in the latter part of the 20th Century with futique nervous systems that have been activated too soon.

STAGE 19, 20, 21: DNA-THINKING AGENTS

A SMALL PERCENT OF POST–SOCIAL HUMAN BEINGS' BRAINS have been activated to the neurogenetic level and can think like DNA. These include the genetic consumers and the genetic engineers. These Agents will find a few hundred thousand from Stages 16, 17, 18 who will immediately respond to neurogenetic signals. These signals appear in the form of sociobiological texts.

WE ARE ROBOTS

REFLECT ON THE SUPER–WONDROUS GLORY of the human brain. The terrestrial human life cycle spins the developing individual through twelve stages. The suckling infant is certainly a very different caste from the serious ten year-old school child. The rock 'n' roll teenager is certainly a different caste from the toddering postmenopausal seniors.

The human being is a robot, blindly operating within the reality bubble of structural caste and current temporal caste imprint. At each developmental stage the individual imprints the current hive reality for that developmental stage. Infants cannot be concerned with teenage sperm-egg fantasies.

EACH GENERATION IS A WAVE MOVING THROUGH THE GENE POOL.

They must suck, suck, suck at the cultural cues that they have imprinted—the touch, smell, taste, and sound of the mother.

Domesticated new-parents at stage eleven suddenly, miraculously forget the barbarian teenage reality in which they lived just a few months previous. Each human accepts the reality of the current temporal stage hive-imprint, and almost totally represses the memory of previous stages.

Hum-ants are directed by involuntary instincts—committed to religious or political passivity, blindly obedient to hive morality—unable to operate as independent individuals.

There is, however, a sizable, and enormously influential population of post-social, self-directed persons swarming on the Western Front. About 15% of those living in the highly developed civilizations of the early 21st Century operate at the post-political level of hedonic consumerism, self-consumerism and self-actualization. They are committed to self-responsible philosophies and do not look to theological or political bureaucrats.

America is the genetic frontier. According to Desmond Morris in his book, *The Naked Ape,* the statistically average American is somewhere between a Neolithic caveman and a

AMERICA IS THE GENETIC FRONTIER. superstitious robot from the priest-run, caste-stratified precivilized Past. The average I.Q. is 100, meaning that the person can read and write primitively, but is generally incapable of any inventive thought. Given a chance, the average American would operate like Attilla the Hun.

The brilliant WoMen who wrote the American Constitution designed a system of checks and balances to keep the average Neolithic American from grabbing control. The Athenian experiment, for example, failed because of Demo-poll—the Tyranny of the Mediocre.

3

CASTES

EVOLUTIONARY AGENTS HAVE WORKED for centuries to decipher the DNA code—to unravel the secrets, techniques and tactics used by the Life-Intelligence to improve our species. This ancient and honorable philosophic specialty has acquired a new professional title—*Ethology*. Ethology studies the survival behavior of living organisms, species and gene pools in their natural environment.

The extraordinary success of humanity is due to the combinatorial complexity of structural and temporal castes in our species. During the Neurogenetic Renaissance (1976-1986) human ethology shot ahead of religion, philosophy, sociology, psychology, personology, astrology, psychiatry and every other primitive system of behavioral theory and practice.

Previous theories of human behavior were regulated to antiquity by the emergence of concepts such as temporal and structural caste in social animals, the key role of migration, population-swarming, hive-limited culture, the emergence of new post-human species, and human robotry.

The Wilson Brothers, Edward and Robert—who performed for psychology what Einstein did for physics—were the parents of this first scientific philosophy. Edward's book, *Sociobiology*, is generally considered the first conscious text on human behavior ever published.

Individual human beings evolve, stage by stage, as higher circuits of the Central Nervous System (CNS) are activated. Post-hive consciousness allows humans to grasp the aesthetics of the DNA blueprint.

THE AIM OF DNA IS TO INCREASE INTELLIGENCE—I^2.

THE GIFT OF DNA

THE GIFT OF DNA is that although we are templated as genetic-robots—structural caste—we are equipped with a 24-caliber brain that allows us to imprint or fabricate every Alpha Reality available to every major life form that preceded us and to imprint every major life form to come.

DNA has given us the equipment to recapitulate-precapitulate the major DNA solutions—past and future. But more than that, DNA has given us access to both CNS and RNA (ribonucleic acid) equipment so that we can creatively re-imprint each of the twenty-four CNS Beta Realities and then restructure our structural caste.

Migration and metamorphosis are obviously effective techniques for improving intelligence (I^2). Migration provides varied territorial options and leads to the growth of musculature and neurotechnology that makes accelerated, accurate locomotion possible. Migration selects for nobility-mobility and thus creates new, more mobile cultures. The young nervous systems of every frontier caste are imprinted with the independent-individuality of migrant Out-Castes.

MOBILITY IS THE CLASSIC STIMULUS FOR INTELLIGENCE INCREASE —I^2.

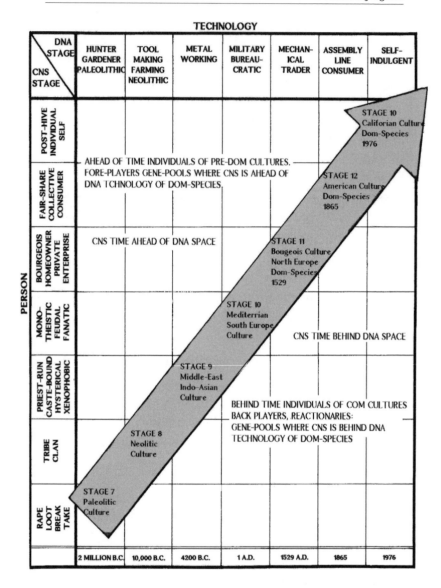

TECHNOLOGY

DNA STAGE / CNS STAGE	HUNTER GARDENER PALEOLITHIC	TOOL MAKING FARMING NEOLITHIC	METAL WORKING	MILITARY BUREAU-CRATIC	MECHAN-ICAL TRADER	ASSEMBLY LINE CONSUMER	SELF-INDULGENT
POST-HIVE INDIVIDUAL SELF							STAGE 10 Califorian Culture Dom-Species 1976
FAIR-SHARE COLLECTIVE CONSUMER	AHEAD OF TIME INDIVIDUALS OF PRE-DOM CULTURES. FORE-PLAYERS GENE-POOLS WHERE CNS IS AHEAD OF DNA TCHNOLOGY OF DOM-SPECIES.				STAGE 12 American Culture Dom-Species 1865		
BOURGEOIS HOMEOWNER PRIVATE ENTERPRISE	CNS TIME AHEAD OF DNA SPACE				STAGE 11 Bougeois Culture North Europe Dom-Species 1529		
MONO-THEISTIC FEUDAL FANATIC				STAGE 10 Mediterrian South Europe Culture		CNS TIME BEHIND DNA SPACE	
PRIEST-RUN CASTE-BOUND HYSTERICAL XENOPHOBIC			STAGE 9 Middle-East Indo-Asian Culture	BEHIND TIME INDIVIDUALS OF COM CULTURES BACK PLAYERS, REACTIONARIES: GENE-POOLS WHERE CNS IS BEHIND DNA TECHNOLOGY OF DOM-SPECIES			
TRIBE CLAN		STAGE 8 Neolitic Culture					
RAPE LOOT BREAK TAKE	STAGE 7 Paleolitic Culture						
	2 MILLION B.C.	10,000 B.C.	4200 B.C.	1 A.D.	1529 A.D.	1865	1976

PERSON

INDIVIDUAL HUMAN BEINGS EVOLVE, STAGE BY STAGE, AS HIGHER CIRCUITS OF THE CENTRAL NERVOUS SYSTEM (CNS) ARE ACTIVATED.

SOCIALIZATION

SOCIALIZATION—the imprinting of harmonious, collaborative behavior—is another tool used by DNA to increase intelligence. A characteristic of advanced socialization is Caste Division—an essential element of socialization and an effective survival device

A species that has developed caste differentiation and enculturation based on multistage imprinting divides into survival specialties—thus complexifying and expanding performance.

The two most successful life forms on this planet—insects and humans—are obvious examples of caste specialization.

CASTE DIFFERENTIATION

Structural Caste defines *Alpha Reality,*
   which is defines genetic hardwiring.

Temporal Caste defines *Beta Reality,*
   which is the developmental staging of
   the wiring.

The most successful-intelligent species manifest both structural and temporal castes. Until our human species understood how these two caste systems work we were unable to understand human psychology and thus unable to manage our own, evolving destiny.

STRUCTURAL CASTE

STRUCTURAL CASTE, OR ALPHA REALITY, involves the genetic division into specialized functions—such as worker hum-ant, warrior hum-ant, drone hum-ant, and builder hum-ant—that characterize hive organisms like social insects   and civilized hum-ants. Structural caste in insects is easily identified by visible morphological— ana-tomical—differences. In humans neurological differ-ences are more impor-tant in determining the behavior of each caste.

Obviously highly complex neuro-logical differences characterize insect hives, It may well be that individual in-sects have more illusions of individuality than we credit them. The nervous systems of juvenile worker-ants are imprinted with specific culture cues. Each corridor of each ant hill has its highly characteristic odors, textures and humidities that identify the inhab-itants. We are reflex-chauvinists when we naively deny that ant hill cultures—100 million years in building—offer their caste members any less sense of individual and hive uniqueness than is offered the average hum-ant. Structural caste is ge-netic-anatomical templating that produces involuntary-robot behaviors. For example, a drone bee looks different from worker bees and queen bees.

CASTE DIVISION IS AN ESSENTIAL ELEMENT OF ADVANCED SOCIALIZATION.

Structural caste differences characterize homo sapiens.

Male and female—is one structural caste difference. Big, muscled, hyper-adrenalized aggressives are a

POLITICALLY REPRESSIVE COUNTRIES FORBID TALK ABOUT GENETIC CASTE-DIFFERENCES

separate caste—the warriors, the Amazons. Dainty, fragile, nurturant minister-types are another caste. Chestmasters like Bobby Fisher, FBI top-cops like J. Edgar Hoover, feisty politicians like Bella Abzug and sex kittens like Marilyn Monroe are caste-exemplars. The caste distinctions are blatantly visible.

It is interesting to note that politically repressive countries forbid talk about genetic caste-differences. Discussion of genetic types is taboo among modern humans. For example, Marxism held that society determined behavior. Caste theories, to a socialist, reek of capital-istic-class-elitist racism. Although politically incorrect, these differences exist nonetheless and were taken for granted by earlier societies.

In western democracies, the Intellectual-Scientist-Caste denies caste differences because of the hive commitment to equality, The revulsion against Nazi, Arab and Zionist genetic fanaticism makes caste discussions *verboten* among liberals—and most scientists are liberals.

DRONE BEES LOOK DIFFERENT FROM WORKER BEES.

By contrast uneducated, lower class people readily accept the reality of racial and caste-differences. Country bumpkins and illiterate farmers are aware of the effects of breeding and thus are far more ethnologically sophisticated than liberal Nobel Prize laureates. Common sense suggests that there are a limited number of basic genetic castes that characterize the human species, and that new caste differences will emerge as homo sapiens continue its accelerated differentiated evolution.

TEMPORAL CASTE

THE MOST IMPRESSIVE AND SUCCESSFUL TECHNIQUE used by DNA to increase the intelligence of social species is temporal caste or *Beta Reality*. Temporal caste refers to the process of maturation in which individuals metamorphosize from one form to another within their life spans. As we pass through developmental stages, we perform different survival functions at each life passage.

Temporal casting in an ant hill assigns to the young the tasks of infant care. Slightly older ants are assigned house keeping and hive-repair functions, metamorphosing into more external functions of exploration, food-gathering and warrior activity.

Reflect on the wondrous neurological advantage of temporal caste. Mature ants know how to perform several caste functions, which means that they must have several gears or circuits in their nervous systems.

An organism that has passed through temporal metamorphic sequences is simply more intelligent.

Temporal caste means polyphase brain and thus multiple Beta Realities. Caterpillar to butterfly; pollywog to frog; pre-teenager to adolescent.

America is the ecological niche of the dominant species—dom-species—and predominant species—predom species—have become an evolutionary pinball machine in which hundreds of genetically different human gene pools and genetic castes bounce around, each caught up in genetic spirals of differing velocities, each fabricating different Technicolor realities and developing new mutational styles in flashing neon.

The most lovable aspect of human temporal casting is that each stage plays a part in the overall 24-element human molecule. Think of the human gene pool as a complex molecule that builds on new elements as it evolves. Temporal casting allows for temporal flexibility. Each generation is a wave moving through the gene pool, contributing to the locomotion of the gene pool through time.

The stage one suckling, floating infant plays an important role in the human ant hill The suckling infant is the glue that holds the enormous technologi- cal civilization to- gether. The infant triggers domestic responses in adults. The baby's task is to suck tits, emit anguished-

DURING PEACETIME TEENAGERS KEEP THE POLICE ESTABLISHMENTS AND THE JUDICIARY GOING. demanding yowls, dirty diapers, and gurgle winningly. The neonate performing its repertoire of activities is working just as hard as the autoworker or the dutiful parent. Sucking mother's breasts turns on hormones that keeps Mom at home.

If Mom's eleventh stage domesticated adult brain is not fed by gurgle cues and cries, the young mother will be down at the dance hall swinging her hips—or, horrors, competing with men. Thus the enormous neurogenetic significance of the Pill. It is no accident that the irresistible Women's Liberation Movement followed the appearance of voluntary birth-control.

Birth control is self-directed management of temporal caste sequence.

Women can postpone maternal-matron-morality. The "youth-cult," that produced middle-aged teeny boppers and married guys sporting Generation X hair styles and wearing satin football hero satin shirts is another by-product of the newly won control of our neurogenetic brain sequences.

School children between the ages of five to eleven years old also play a crucial role in the human hive. Young students keep the enormous educational industry going. Schools become bureaucratic paper-factories keeping teachers busy, school administrators occupied, and counselors engaged. The whole insectoid apparatus is designed to imprint the young robots with role-models, making them ready to take their places in a bureaucratic-socialist centralized hive civilization where everyone is trained to play a role.

The Barbarian Teenager Caste similarly plays a vital role in the human anthill by providing warriors in times of war. Indeed, teenagers encourage war.

Every dictator knows that the way to keep the restless students from rioting in the university is to get them fighting on the border.

In times of peace the crime rate rises. More than half of all reported crimes are committed by those under eighteen. During peace time the task of teenagers is to keep the police establishment and the judiciary going. If unreported vandalisms, bloodletting fights and hubcap coups were included, we would see that 90% of all crimes are committed by barbarian teenag-

EVERY CASTE HAS TO BE KEPT OCCUPIED.

ers or unmarried, pre-domestic males. If adolescence were eliminated from the human cycle, there would be no Red Brigades, no rock-concert riots. The monolithic police bureaucracy would immediately crumble and in its anguished collapse would take the entire society down with it. Every caste has to be kept occupied.

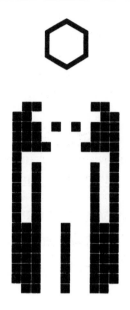

It is more comfortable for us to understand human robot-hood by looking at others. Thus we notice that in "primitive" tribes young children perform baby-care. Older girls help with agriculture while older boys guard the flocks. After puberty temporal caste assignments change dramatically. In all societies adolescent males pass through a warrior stage.

In civilized societies technology and complex labor divisions have diminished the survival value of child-castes. Thus the elaborate culture of organized play and extended education to prepare youngsters for warrior and post-warrior status.

WE ARE ALL UFOS

WE DO NOT HAVE TO LOOK ALOFT TO FLYING SAUCERS to find alien intelligence. We are all UFOs—Unidentified Flying Organisms. The first step in interspecies diplomacy is to recognize the species differences among us, exchange basic vocabulary cues as to each other's realities and establish interspecies diplomatic courtesies so that the womb-planet Earth can be shared harmoniously, and abandoned gracefully. Then new plan-its, carefully designed to fit the differing realities of different species, can be fabricated in High Orbit.

To keep American hivers from understanding the blunt facts about genetic robot-hood, human castes produce public relations experts, sometimes called philosophers or theologians. From the evolutionary point of view, philosophy is post-hive human ethology. The task of an ethological philosopher is to define the different species of humans and to explain how they interact to assure the survival of the gene pool and of each caste.

PHILOSOPHY IS POST-HIVE HUMAN ETHOLOGY.

The dom-species is not yet ready for that. The caste spokespersons for each caste describes reality from the perspective of their species. Since each caste inhabits a very different reality, moral outrage is endemic—Blacks, Gays, Holocaust obsessed Zionists, right-wingers, irate homeowners.

Each caste lives in a different time zone. The dogma of the Paleolithic did not work in technological America, but this did not discourage the attempt by our species to impose its hunter-gatherer reality on others. Most bewildered are the retiring liberal humanists who keep shouting: "We are all one! Brotherhood of Man! We are all equal and homogenous."

Genetic heterogeneity has, of course, always been obvious to those geared to look for it.

As you walk through the forest you don't expect
each species you meet to be the same or to play
survival games by your rules. The insightful etholo-
gist admires each lifestyle—the radar speed of a
rabbit, the innocent grace of a wolf, the levity of a
bird, the sincere cunning of a spider. The same
honor can be extended to each human caste you
meet as you swim through the urban coral reef.

The next eleven people you meet probably belong to eleven different species in mutation— living in different time zones, at different levels of contelligence.

4

OUR TERRESTRIAL GOD

THE JUDEO-CHRISTIAN BIBLE is an invaluable index to the neurogenetic level of the period in which it was written. The genetic stage of a gene pool can be identified by the personality characteristics of the Local God.

Jehovah of Genesis is a low-level barbarian macho punk God. He boastfully claims to have created the heaven and the stars and the world, but provides no technical details or replicable blueprints. His preoccupations, whims, anxieties, jealousies, rules and hatred of women are primitive mammalian brain. His petty prides are primate.

He is very animal-territorial. He owns the Garden—this Mafia Capo Jehovah—and allows Adam and Eve their tenancy there. He has the right to throw them out. He puts his warrior guards on the periphery of His turf to scare off intruders. Jehovah exemplifies stage five demanding with the intelligence of a Lion or a possessive child.

JEHOVAH OF GENESIS IS A MACHO PUNK GOD.

A post-terrestrial God would not be concerned with possession of territory. Such a DNA ecological-engineer God would understand that all creatures must evolve through the marine, territorial, artifact, and social technologies and that they must self-actualize at each evolution, passing the second stage infant fish-brained mentality, the fifth stage mammalian-brained demanding, the eight stage detailed-brained pedantic juvenile and eleventh stage domesticated adult, as well as those advanced stages of self-defined divinity.

Wise parents smile when their little cub says, "My...and mine" because it is the beginning of the definition of reality and self in terms of territory. Every wise parent smiles praise when the little stage eight detailed-brain juvenile humanoid proudly presents a crayon drawing or some original sym-bolic creation. It is true that terrestrial parents get

upset when the kids fool around with the Tree of Good and Evil—the socio-sex rituals of the local hive—but this is no reason to throw the kids out of the house and put a flaming torch at the front door to keep the poor errant youngster from contritely creeping back. The Jehovah God has not reached the technological level or the civilized stage of parental cultural transmission.

The fact that sexuality is not a concern of the Genesis supports the suggestion that in this folk legend we are dealing with the reality of a seventh stage parrot-brained Paleolithic-herding tribe obsessed with territory—moving uneasily into an eight stage inventive self-actualization brain. Thus, the *Bible* is revealed to be a collection of histories and taboos produced by backward, Sematic tribes, pre-civilized, in awe and fear of the sexually active feudal kingdoms around them.

The power of the Bible-thumping Christianities that emerged from the Old Testament tradition is rural, pre-urban. Fundamentalist Christianity appeals to pre-civilized, prudish tribal people who are not ready for urban feudal pleasures.

The *Bible* becomes a valuable ethological document to help us locate the evolutionary stage which emerged in the Middle East at biblical times. The Principle of Correspondence keeps us from rejecting the Judeo-Christian Bible as erroneous.

CORRESPONDENCE THEORY

THE CORRESPONDENCE PRINCIPLE REQUIRES that every new theory contain a limiting transition to the old theory it replaces. Insofar as the old theory has fitted some sound experiments, the new theory must concur. If Planck's constant h tends towards zero, the quantum equations become just the classical ones. If the speed of light approaches infinity, Einstein's kinematic and dynamical equations go over to Newton's, and so on over a large number of examples from contemporary physics.

As we apply the Correspondence Principle to sociobiology and exo-psychology, we expect that each new Einsteinian, relativistic theory of human behavior and neurogenetic evolution will include a translation back to the old theory it replaced. Darwinians are clearly in violation when they fanatically, summarily reject the Monotheistic Creation theories of the Judeo-Christian Bible. Newer theories of evolution must provide new insights into the validity of the older theories—specifying the historical, neurotechnical factors which limited the earlier metaphors. Any new theory of neurogenetics must relate to and lovingly demonstrate why the previous philosophic theory was "right" for its time arid its gene-pool—knowing that those to come will affectionately do the same for our theories.

The astrological Zodiac which has continued to attract the attentions of intelligent people for five thousand years must have some caste-type meaning—and this significance must be explained by the theories which improve it.

MEDIEVAL ALCHEMY AND ASTROLOGY WERE NOT BLUNDERS REPUDIATED BY DOW CHEMICAL AND FREUD.

New theories can improve, can explain, but not reject, the Zodiac. The Genesis version of Creation obviously must have had profound survival validity even though it obviously fails to take into account the newer evidence from Darwinian, Mendelian, DNA, sociobiological and behavior genetics.

Correspondence Theory is a "magic stick" for searching out new laws, because it sets formal constraints on the new mathematics. As Morrison emphasizes, the Correspondence Principle secures science against the loss of achievements of the past. For innovators it is a warning like the Hippocratic maxim for physicians—above all do no harm! Classical mechanics is not a mere blunder that was repudiated in 1905, as the headlines imply.

This affectionate maxim holds even more strongly for human ethology—i.e., philosophy. All the theological and philosophical systems of the past must be seen as attempts, valid at the preceding, more primitive stage of neurotechnology, to explain the inner-outer (CNS-DNA) reality paradox.

Thus the concern in the Starseed Transmissions (See my books, *Neurologic, Terra II, What Does WoMan Want?, Exo-psychology, Neuropolitics, Game of Life, Neurological Tarot*) to trace correspondences among the many occult theories of the past, including Christianity and Buddhism, and the newer sciences. Each past philosophy, far from being repudiated, or rejected, joyously fits into an evolving, stage-by-stage theory. Medieval alchemy and astrology were not blunders repudiated by Dow Chemical and Freud.

BEWARE OF MONOTHEISM

THERE IS ONE GOD AND HIS NAME IS _____ (substitute Hive-Label). If there is only One God then there is no choice, no option, no selection of reality. There is only submission or heresy.

The word Islam means "submission." The basic posture of Christianity is kneeling—Thy will be done.

Beware of Monotheism

Monotheism is the primitive religion that centers human consciousness on hive authority.

Monotheism satisfies hive-oriented terrestrials such as barbarian teenagers, domesticated adults, and retiring elders, who eagerly seek to layoff responsibility on some Big Boss. By contrast, monotheism does profound mischief to those who are evolving to post-hive stages of reality. Advanced mutants, operating at stages thirteen to eighteen, do make the discovery that "All is One," as the realization dawns that "My Brain creates all the realities that I experience." The discovery of Self is frightening because the novitiate possessor of the automobile body and the automobile brain must accept all the power that the hive religions attributed to jealous Jehovah.

The First Commandment of all monotheisms is—I am the Lord, thy God. Thou shall have no other Gods before me. All monotheisms are vengeful, aggressive, expansionist, intolerant.

Stage 10 Barbarian Teenagers—Islam-Catholicism

Stage 11 Domesticated Adults—Protestant Evangelism

Stage 12 Retiring Elders—Communist Imperialism.

A monotheist's duty is to destroy any competitive heresy. Concepts such as devil, hell, guilt, eternal damnation, sin, evil are fabricators by the hive to insure loyalty to Hive Central.

These doctrines are precisely designed to intimidate and crush individualism.

The process of mutating into self-hood plunges the mutant into a crossfire of neurogenetic moral flak. Most of the freak-outs, bad trips and hellish experiences are caused by monotheistic morality. However, it must be emphasized that monotheism is a necessary stage. Monotheism is a technology—a tool—to bring pre-civilized tribes people and caste-segregated primitives into the collectives necessary to develop the post-hive, post-terrestrial technologies.

A major evolutionary step is taken when the individual says: "There is only one God who creates the universe. This God is my Brain. As the driver of this Brain I have created a universe in which there are innumerable other Gods of equal post-hive autonomy with whom I seek to interest. And my universe was, itself, created by a higher level of divinity—DNA—whose mysteries and wonders I seek to understand and harmonize with."

YOUR
BRAIN
IS GOD.

5

PATHOLOGY PRECEDES POTENTIAL

THE TERM *GENETIC COUNSELING* INDICATES that a genetic consumer consciousness is dawning. The emphasis is on genetic *disorder*, not upon genetic *endowment*, but this is to be expected. A new technology always appeals to hive-security first as a way of dealing with danger. Awareness of genetic disorder precedes

GENETIC CAUSES EXIST FOR HUMAN PROBLEMS.

awareness of genetic excellence, just as psychiatry precedes self-actualized psychology. Pathology precedes potential. When the experts in a hive begin treating "broken-down personalities" they have recognized the existence of "personality." The next step is for healthy individuals to take charge of their own "selfs."

New technology always appeals to hive-security first.

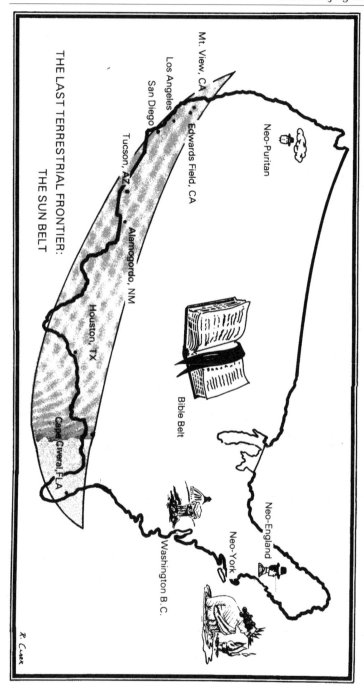

THE LAST TERRESTRIAL FRONTIER:
THE SUN BELT

Mt. View, CA
Los Angeles
San Diego
Edwards Field, CA
Tucson, AZ
Alamogordo, NM
Houston, TX
Cape Civeral, FLA

Neo-Puritan

Bible Belt

Washington B.C.
Neo-York
Neo-England

R. Clark

The following course was found among the classes offered by a prestigious Sun Belt University. "The Ad Hoc Committee on Genetic Counseling of the American Society of Human Genetics described genetic counseling as a 'communication process which deals with the human problems associated with the occurrence, or the risk of occurrence, of a genetic disorder in the family.' This one-day workshop is primarily for health professionals who want to learn how to do genetic counseling or who want to strengthen their skills in this field."

Hidden in this course description are valuable neurogenetic clues, evolutionary evidence, which is easily overlooked by hive observers because it reveals much about the neurogenetic stage of the hive culture—and of the planet.

Genetic counseling appeared a generation after personality counseling. When an advanced, post-political culture offers courses in "Job Counseling," "Personality Counseling" or "Marital Counseling," Evolutionary Agents know that a move towards self-actualization is occurring—a free-mobile-individually oriented society is emerging.

SELF-DISCOVERY

THE YOUNGER GENERATION IS GENERALLY VIEWED as being too laid back, apathetic, narcissistic, self-indulgent, and sensual. There are periods when a species or an individual or a nation needs to lay back, mellow out, cocoon-quiescent and recoup. Intelligent pursuit of happiness is a challenge of the human experience. However, this quiescence is more apparent than real.

SELF ACTUALIZATION PRECEDES INTERPERSONAL FUSION

The latter 20th Century was a period of *self-discovery*—a daring assertion of personal pleasure rather than societal reward.

We've been in an unprecedented era of *self-actualization.* Young people and most intelligent older people who appear to be laid back are taking care of their own situation first. They are "getting their heads together," discovering and tending their bodies, learning how to produce their reality movies. College students aren't charging after partisan dogmas or idealistic rhetoric. But don't be deceived by this quiescence. It denotes neither apathy nor stupidity. In fact, it may well be the better part of wisdom to lay back until something worthy of your intelligence comes along.

GENETIC INTELLIGENCE

THE SELF-ACTUALIZATION MOVEMENT ORIGINATED—where all individual freedoms start—on the Western Frontier. On nursery planets the military warrior-caste is responsible for developing new technologies for faster mobility and communication. Soon afterwards, the citizens in the Western Frontier co-opt the technology for their own actualization.

Generic causes exist for human problems. Discovering this is a big breakthrough—resisted, of course, by stage twelve retiring socialist demo-poll cultures. Genetic determination focuses on gene pool statistics and caste-differentiation, thus minimizing the importance of hive managers. Socialist-welfare cultures insist that the collective super-hive—also known as "The State"—assume responsibility for everything.

When we humans begin to face the fact that genes determine the varied destiny of our different children, then we are ready to see that genes determine our own caste. Next comes the catastrophic discovery that each gene pool is a time-hive, a genetic molecule, made up of many elements called "castes" and that the whole game is genetic robotry.

After genetic counseling courses began studying genetic problems courses in genetic potentials and self-selected breeding soon emerged on the Western Frontier. **THE WHOLE GAME IS GENETIC ROBOTRY.** Neither China or the now defunct Soviet Union offered courses on genetic elites. As our intelligence evolves the definition of genetic counseling will evolve from an emphasis on pathology to one of excellence and growth.

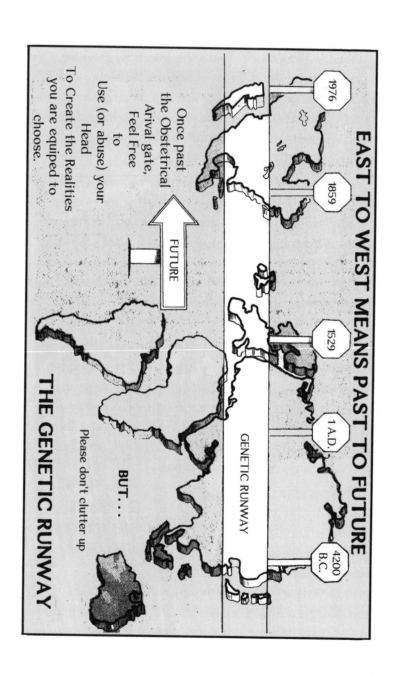

EAST TO WEST MEANS PAST TO FUTURE

1976 1859 1529 1 A.D. 4200 B.C.

GENETIC RUNWAY

FUTURE

Once past
the Obstetrical
Arival gate,
Feel Free
to
Use (or abuse) your
Head
To Create the Realities
you are equiped to
choose.

BUT....

Please don't clutter up

THE GENETIC RUNWAY

The definition of genetic counseling might read like this: "A communication process which deals with the human *potentials* associated with the occurrence, or the possibility of occurrence, of a genetic *advance* in the gene pool." The dom-species on the Sunset Strip move from stage twelve social-sacrifice to stage thirteen self-consumerism.

PreDom Ideas Emerging On The Western Frontier

STAGE 14: Self-Actualized Adults

Bodily Intelligence Self-Actualization "My Body is my Time Ship"

STAGE 15: Hedonic Networkers

Voluntary Civilian Space Migration "We Are Not Terrestrials"

STAGE 16: Brain-Reality Consumer

Brain Reality Consumerism "I Can Select My Own Reality"

STAGE 17: Brain Reality Self-Actualized

Brain Reality Self-Actualism "I Can Create My Own Reality"

STAGE 18: Brain Reality Fusion

Brain Reality Fusion "We Can Fabricate an External Reality"

STAGE 19: Genetic Consumer

Genetic Consumerism "I Can Select My Own Genetic Reality"

STAGE 20: Genetic Engineer

Genetic Engineering "I Can Fabricate My Own Genetic Reality"

Terrestrial dom-species place all notions of the future under hive-taboo. The ideas of bodily-sensory-hedonic consumerism—fiercely taboo in domesticated adults and retiring elder societies—crumbled by the late 20th Century on the Western Frontier. The predom self-actualized adult stage taboo against bodily self-actualization similarly crumbled—as exemplified by the legalization of marijuana, the classic tool of one who wishes to control one's own hedonic reality.

The predom hedonic networker taboo of the late 20th Century condemned civilian space migration. The Director of NASA, Dr. Frosch, testified in Congress that civilian space migration was a "preadolescent" idea and he was precisely correct. If preadolescence is defined as age eleven, then a preadolescent idea will become a young-voter idea in seven years and will be legalized in California ten years later.

TABOOS

THE DOM-SPECIES IMPOSE TWO SETS OF TABOOS to maintain its equilibrium and hive-solidarity—exdom taboos condemn the past and predom taboos condemn the future. In other words, the dom-species is held together by its opposition to the proximal past and future stages.

The shames attached to cannibalism, violence, violation of property, dishonesty, and rape are examples of exdom taboos. The Ten Commandments are a valuable index of the neurogenetic stage of the time. Thou shall honor thy parents; Thou shall not steal, kill, lie, sexually trespass, or violate territory within the hive. Thou shall adore the hive-totem and not worship past pagan Gods or Future Gods.

TODAY'S NEW TABOO IS TOMORROW'S ADVANCE

Social welfare countries, exemplified by retiring elders, place under taboo all forms of individuality—both past and future. Domesticated adults societ-ies—the democratic-bourgeois—place under taboo stage ten barbarian teenager feudal elitism as well as the retiring elders state power brains and Me-generation grown-up post-familial individuality.

The predom brain-reality consumer taboo in the latter 20th Century condemned intervention into brain control—either by others or self. Thus the revulsion against CIA brain experiments using drugs or bioelectrical means. The predom self-actualized brain reality taboo against self-directed brain change was even more rigid. While there was some liberal hand-wringing about CIA experiments with LSD, there was stark terror at the thought of self-appointed individuals using psychedelic drugs to change their *own* realities.

The predom accelerated brain reality fused taboo against intentional communes of individuals linking to create new realities was very pervasive in the 20th Century. Every attempt to construct such communities was routinely snuffed.

Taboo Revelations

THE PREDOM TABOO AGAINST GENETIC CONSUMERISM surfaced when citizens became morally outraged by genetic engineering and cloning. The emergence of a new taboo is always sign for evolutionary rejoicing. Today's new taboo is tomorrow's advance. Agents who create new crimes are automatically promoted to the Gut-Caste Hall of Fame. Examples of relatively new crimes include bootleg radio broadcasting, psychedelic drug manufacturing, nuclear research, computer larceny, leaving a country without an exit visa, DNA research, and cloning.

Up-Set the Dom-Species

THE FLAP OVER RECOMBINANT DNA RESEARCH, life extension and cloning is a wonderful sign that neurogenetic consciousness is emerging. Nothing can happen in evolution until the dom-species gets upset and worried. When the redneck politicians and the liberal agitators moralize about "monsters escaping from the laboratory and being unleashed on the unsuspecting public," the out-caste intelligence operative perks up interest. The "monsters," of course, are us in the future.

Nothing can happen in evolution until the dom-species gets upset.

Evolutionary Agents reassure the dom-species about future-phobias and point out that allowing the next mutation to occur is the best way to avoid past terrors, because past-terrors are worse than future fears. Thus domesticated adult capitalists realized that some social-welfarism is the only way to avoid a return to barbarian-dictatorships. The communist stage ten dictators realized that some individual consumerism is the only way to avoid a return to tribal anarchy.

It is the Evolutionary Agents' role to demonstrate that civilian voluntary space migration is the only way to deal with the tensions of nationalism, tribalism and self-actualization. Similarly, homophobes come to see that the only way to keep homosexuals away from their children is to allow gay societies in post-terrestrial plan-its. Racists of all colors realize that the only way to preserve discrimination and racial pride is in High Orbital Mini Earths—HOMEs.

It is becoming obvious that the only solution to hive terrors, both past and future, is migration to space plan-its. The past always migrates behind the future. Today's future taboo is tomorrow's dogma.

Liberals are alarmed that nuclear energy, brain-changing drugs, radiation-control of brains, genetic engineering might fall into the hands of barbarian territorial dictators. Cloning, the key migratory technique for a post-terrestrial species, was first discussed in fearful terms of Hitler-like revivals. The hive custodians frighten people with mad scientist Nazi-devil rumors and thus concealed the possibility that you can clone yourself and friends. The same taboo-terror is projected on post-terrestrial intelligence. We are warned that Martians were coming to harm us—not to enlighten or entertain us.

TODAY'S FUTURE TABOO IS TOMORROW'S DOGMA.

Such natural hive fears can be assuaged by the realization that nuclear energy, brain-changing drugs such as LSD, cloning, and genetic research can only be safely employed in frontier, experimental communities—which can be found only in **HIGH ORBITAL** HOMEs. The first signs of **MIGRATION IS** neurogenetic consciousness are communities that are into self- **BEGINNING.** actualization and states where the governors are space plan-it enthusiasts.

NEUROTECHNOLOGICAL MUTATION

THE HUMAN BRAIN IS PROGRAMMED by RNA-DNA to fabricate technological realities and to build environments and new plan-its. External technology produces the pollution that activates the next brain-circuit.

DNA is not concerned with evolving new anatomical-physiological forms adapted to a heavy 1-G planet. Terrestrial evolution is over—irrelevant. Now that high orbital migration is beginning, now that the futique species are moving into their designated ecological niche— high orbit—the goal of DNA is to create technologies adapted to multiple-G living

DNA is an evolutionary acceleration tool.

The current survival problems on planet Earth are due to overpopulation swarming and cannot be solved by anatomical mutations. The next stages are neurological— neurotechnological. Encourage the appropriate castes of the human species to decode DNA and increase altitude and mobility.

EVOLUTIONARY AGENTS' CALL TO ARMS

LIFE IS NO LONGER A DISASTER MOVIE. The Who-Done-It mystery is solved! You are responsible. You are the hip-robots who are going to take over the Master-Designer role. It is your job to fabricate improved mini-worlds. Who are you? You are those who recognize this signal and self-select yourselves as Future Builders.

6

THE PLEASURE CASTE

THE PLEASURE CASTE is a strange and powerful caste of humans whose psychology and neurology has been ignored by philosophers because of the taboo nature of the subject—pleasure, beauty, sensuality, and eroticism.

History reveals that each gene pool and every successful civilization has produced an aesthetic-elite caste—those whose nervous systems are especially sensitive to sensual stimulation; those who have the ability to receive, manage and transmit neurosomatic, hedonic signals; those who are robot-programmed to stimulate pleasure in themselves and in others—either singularly or in cooperation with other reality-artists.

AESTHETIC-ARTIST-SENSORY CASTES

Hedonic Consumers—those who receive pleasure.

Hedonic Directors—those who create pleasure realities for themselves and others.

Hedonic Producers—those who exchange pleasure.

The pleasure industry includes those called artists—show business people, entertainers, and courte-
sans. Hive philosophers and establishment reality-
definers tend to discredit the Pleasure-Aesthetic
Castes and the contribu-
tions they make to
the species. There
is little overt,
bureaucratic
pressure on young
people to take up
a life of courtesan-
actress-musician-
artist when they "grow
up." Indeed, the classic situation calls for discouragement by the gene pool of such aspirations on the part
of the young. However, at the same time that the
hedonic occupations are publicly taboo, there is a
covert acceptance of them as evidenced by the pervasive presence of the show-biz-pleasure profession.
Nightclubs, saloons, theatres, carnivals, brothels,
dance halls—however fake, tinsel, laundered the actual
performance—the allure, the promise is always the
same. Somatic reward, inhuman soft-skin-bliss, hip
sophistication, erotic movement, hedonic consumption
of self-indulgence and self-actualization.

GENETIC CASTE

WITH ESTABLISHED SOCIETY actively discouraging recruit-
ment into the pleasure professions, how do we account for the fact that in every gene pool and in every
age a certain percentage of young adults pop up as
pleasure-dispensers? The answer is found in genetic
caste. Good looks and animal magnetism are the

giveaways. Observe any group of children at play and you can forecast those who are robot-templated by DNA to play hedonic roles, who give off the sexual radiation and the flamboyant self-confidence of the budding performer.

An interesting dilemma appears at this point. We do not have a formal, precise language to classify and describe the various pleasure-roles and hedonic processes. Indeed, before *The Principles and Practice of Hedonic Psychology* was written there had been little scholarly attention to pleasure in Western literature. Whereas there exists an enormous nosology or disease classification of pain, an endless clinical listing of negative pathological states.

There is no psychiatric or psychological classification of the states of excellence, elite accomplishment, or pleasure.

It is true that a crude literature of beauty-pleasure exists in the Orient—pillow books, Tantric Hindu texts, and Islamic-Sufi works. Neurocensorship is why there is no terminology for beauty-pleasure in the West. If words are invented for these myriad hedonic delights, then people will talk about them and enjoy them—a turn of events which Christian-Marxist hive establishments can not tolerate.

Before the 1960s, in Western culture, hedonic bliss was taboo—reserved only for the aristocracy. Sexual pleasure was limited to marital intercourse—and then only for hive reproductive purposes. The taboo against the recognition of pleasure began to crumble in the 1960s and for the first time in the history of humanity a mass middle-class awakened to self-actualized hedonism. We can justly use the term "awaken" to describe the sudden insight that the body is a pleasure instrument, designed to receive a wide range of sensory stimuli that can be self-directed and self-controlled.

THE BODY IS A PLEASURE INSTRUMENT,

AESTHETIC ARTIST SENSORY CASTES

Hedonic Consumer—those who receive pleasure.

Hedonic Director—those who create pleasure realities for themselves and others.

Hedonic Producer—those who exchange pleasure.

PLEASURE AND SATISFACTION

HIVE-MORALISTS FOR MILLENNIA HAVE LAMENTED the innate, pervasive tendency of human beings to kick-out in bursts of irrationality and pleasure seeking. It is looked on as extra-social self-indulgence. There is a distinction between two very different hedonic reactions. *Pleasures* are hedonic experiences caused by activating higher-faster-future brains at the service of and controlled by self. *Satisfactions* are intoxication and narcotic escape experiences caused by activating slower-lower past circuits.

EACH CIVILIZATION PRODUCES RITUALISTIC DRUG TAKING TO ALLOW TEMPORARY ANIMAL REVERSION. Both experiences take consciousness away from domesticated robot-hood. Pleasures move one up from hive routine into the self-actualized future. Intoxicants, tranquilizers and narcotics move one back to the past—down from domestication, to primate and mammalian instinctual satisfactions.

Civilized terrestrial humans, robotically and blindly harnessed to species tasks, and dependent upon gene-hive rewards for duty well-done, need to slowdown, turnoff, escape domesticated pressure. Boredom and social inefficiency would result without some sequential opportunity to regress from hive morality, to activate the primitive circuits of the brain. Intoxicants and narcotic escapes are built-in devices to allow ritual regression to earlier, lower, slower stages. That they are conventionally naughty is their power and delight.

RITUALISTIC DRUG TAKING

THE DUTIFUL DOMESTICATED ADULT BRAIN and the retiring elder brain insectoids live in a reality centered upon hive duty. The ten earlier brains are there, but are taboo, often blanked from consciousness. Brains are turned on and off by means of neurotransmitter chemicals. Civilization provides ritualistic means of allowing reactivation of the earlier brains—temporarily naughty immorality, programmed animalism—permissible retrogression in every successful eleventh and twelfth stage domesticated adult and retiring elder brain

Each civilization produces ritualistic drug taking which allows temporary animalistic reversion. This process is best seen in the Japanese culture—surely the most insectoid society in world history. The Japanese have developed ritualistic drunkenness which permits even the most dutiful to regress to animalism as seen in stages four to six—rodent-brained toddlers, mammalian-brained demanding kids, and monkey-brained territorial children.

The German culture, another highly domesti-cated-duty society also allows its citizens a sched-uled intoxication-regression in the Fasching-Carni-val. Even the sober, tidy Swiss permit each other a Springtime return to pseudo-bestiality when these paragons of the domesticated adult get tipsy and lurch around like sodden bears shamelessly littering the streets of Basel with confetti! Masks are worn

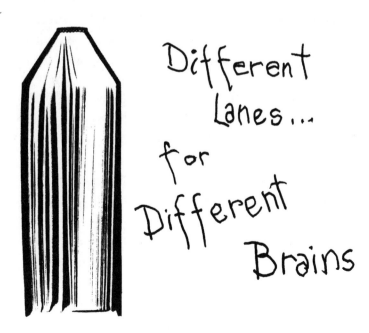

Different Lanes...
for
Different Brains

means

CENTRAL
NERVOUS
SYSTEM

your best friend!

don't leave home
without it

■   ■   ■

at these carnival regressions—the Burghers do not want to have their inner animals seen.

Other methods for ceremonial return of the animal-brain-stages involve totems exhibited at athletic events, parades, and social gatherings. The unrepressed emotions released at these events are not sexual, however. Genital satisfaction is not the central motive. Middle-age, middle-class folks return to preadolescence and become exhibitionistic monkeys or noisy, often savage mammals as when thousands of spectators engage in physical violence directed against the territorial rival in soccer games around the world, for example

The orchestrated revival of earlier brains is a basic issue in any stable gene pool. Each of our twelve terrestrial brains has its own ego, demands activation and must be allowed to cut loose on some regular basis. The best-run civilizations have worked out a weekly return of the regressed. Domesticated adults work dutifully Monday through Friday. On Saturday they are allowed to assemble in animal-totem competitions—the Bulldogs of Yale versus the Horned Toads of Texas Christian. Saturday night the socially approved intoxicant is imbibed, permitting a temporary explosion of mammalian territorial competition and sexual low-jinks. Sunday morning the chastened and hung-over domesticate attends a DNA adoration ceremony in which the dignified gene-hive Creator is recognized, the brief foray back to animalism exorcised. Purged and reborn, the domesticate adult hum-ant is ready to start the next week of hive duty.

Narcotics

ALCOHOL TRIGGERS MAMMALIAN REACTIONS. Another powerful set of neurotransmitters reconstruct even more primitive realities. Narcotics reactivate first stage newly born amoeboid-like brain experiences and put the domesticate in touch with relaxed, floating, vegetative pre-terrestrial-marine neurological realities.

Narcotic drugs are approved when used in sickness rituals. Symptomatic cries for help can stimulate shaman-doctors to offer the narcotic experience which activates lower-brain consciousness—ancient, infantile, vegetative. The taboo is necessary for maintaining hive discipline. The narcotic return to marine status is so tempting, so inviting, that it must be administered by an authority figure. The domesticate is not allowed access to first circuit neurotransmitters—chemical substances, such as acetylcholine or dopamine, that transmit nerve impulses across a synapse. Self-administration of narcotics to actualize infantile responses are not tolerated for fear that everyone will reject the busy, hectic, adult demands of the hive and escape back to vegetative-ocean bliss. The Doctor Ceremony is the method by which hive-society allows citizens to plug back into the early marine circuits.

Intoxicant-narcotic behavior engages earlier-slower-lower brains; hedonic behavior engages future circuits.

An amusing diagnostic sidelight on domesticated terrestrial civilizations is that it is acceptable to phone-in sick to the office and thus avoid work. Hive-society recognizes that the insectoid slavery it imposes is basically lethal to the workers. Consequently, the ceremony of sick leave is allowed.

It is impossible, however, to phone-in "well" to the hive-center to announce: "I feel so good today, I'm not coming in to work." In the hedonic society of the future—when the dom-species is a fourth stage self-actualized adult—provision will be made for "well leave" in addition to "sick leave."

The difference between intoxicant-narcotic behavior and hedonic behavior should now be clear. The former engages earlier-slower-lower instinctual brains. The latter moves consciousness and behavior into the self-actualized future, engages future neural circuits. The former are rewards for the overworked domesticate. The latter are genetic endowments, new brains presented, ready-or-not, by the evolutionary process—not earned, but grown-into.

7

OUT OF THE CLOSET

T HE NEW CULTURE WHICH EMERGED from the 1960s was fabricated by newly activated teenage nervous systems. These nervous systems had been imprinted by signals urging self-indulgence, self-discovery and self-actualization. This generation was caste-out far beyond hive limits where reputations, and at times, bodies were placed on the lines, The first benefit of this out-caste behavior was that college education is better today.

There is a caste which benefits from anger and stirring up trouble. It is called the legal profession.

Left-wing lawyers say, "Well, what's wrong with the college students today? They are not angry as they were in the 1960s." Well, of course, they are not. Because in the 1960s we had some very irritable and irritating bureaucrats running the colleges, and running the country. Fortunately, this has changed.

You have no idea how insectoid things were in the college scene in the mid-20th Century. You may not remember back to the dark, ancient days of Eisenhower and McCarthy and Neil Sedaka and Elvis Presley. At that time college administrators, college presidents and college professors were considered to be in loco-parents, which meant it was their job to act as parents to keep the boys and girls apart!

Matrons checked women in and out of the dormitories to make sure that the inevitable did not happen—sperm-egg connection.

Today there is more understanding, tolerance and awareness between the generations. The Out-Castes of the 1960s have become the dom-species of the Sunset Strip. These parents were the young-sters of the 1960s. College instructors, policemen and the bank executives were hippies.

People running the country, lived through the 1960s as long-haired dissidents and had that testing experience of opposition to the power-authority gang. They are more tolerant of, sometimes even supportive of, differences—the sign of a secure, genetically sophisticated species.

Young people enjoy a certain serenity and relaxation that wasn't possible before the 1960s. Young people are freer because those before them, the previous sperm-egg wave, fought hard to end that unneces-sary quiver of hive-paranoia—the peace time draft.

Some people say these cultural changes are phases, temporary hula hoop fads. But they aren't. You can't go back. The cultural changes of the 1960s are irreversible. Certainly the sexual revolution which activated empathy and understanding between men and women will never be repealed.

THE CULTURAL CHANGES OF THE 1960S ARE IRREVERSIBLE.

SEXUAL MUTATION

THERE ARE MANY ASPECTS OF THE SEXUAL MUTATION. First, there is enhancement of sexual activity. Some older hive sociologists complain: "What is all this sex talk about? *Reader's Digest* and advice columnists assure us that people were making out in the 1950s and 1940s as much as you are." Well, maybe. The quantity of sexual relations may not have changed, but I am assure you that the quality of sexual relationships has changed. There is an intelligence and an aesthetic sensitivity—a tender understanding, a playfulness that simply didn't exist before the sexual revolution of the 1960s.

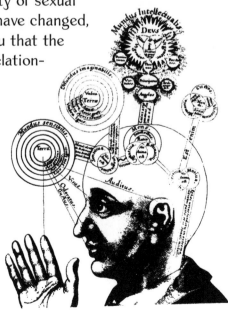

Another aspect of the sexual revolution has to do with the relationship among and between the sexes. Certainly there can be no return to the romantic-feudal situation in which both men and women were going through the robot charade of macho-femme-fatale sexual impersonation. There is a wiser acceptance now of the electric difference between the basic equality of and the necessity for an intelligent and exquisite fusion among the sexes.

The sexual revolution was an intelligence-raising movement. It was a neurological revolution with two aspects—body activation and brain actualization.

THE BRAIN IS EMERGING FROM THE CLOSET

THE NOTION OF SELF-DIRECTED BRAIN CHANGE didn't exist in the late 1950s and early 1960s. It was necessary to turn people on to this option. Evolutionary Agents were robot-programmed to perform this activation role, sending a futique signal to nervous systems. If they are ready for it, if the time is right and the signal is precise—ZAP! The new circuits will activate! People will open up like flowers in May—which is what happened in the 1960s.

Remember this notion of bodily awareness was a predom-species concept in the 1950s. Before 1960 hive wisdom held that the body was an instrument designed for reproductive purposes. Sure, you were allowed to jump up and down on each other on Saturday night for breeding purposes—instinctual sperm-egg exchange.

The notion of intelligent pleasure, hedonic engineering, bodily self-direction, didn't exist. The notions of consciousness raising and body awareness and personal growth did not exist.

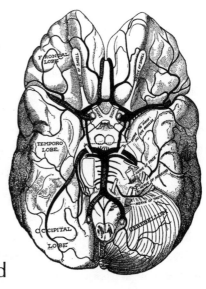

Of course you know what happened. Since the 1960s the consciousness-pleasure hedonic-intelligence business has become the largest industry in the country. The Great American Consumer Society has co-opted the notion of "feel good." And that's a step forward. Nothing is wrong with hedonic consumerism. It was bound to happen. It's a stage, of course. New ideas always get watered down and vulgarized. In every gene-pool, every caste is going to pick up on new energies. So, let us face the amusing fact. The self-directed pleasure business has become an American obsession.

There is an enormous hedonic industry in this country which simply did not exist in the 1950s. We have water beds, satin sheets, diets, health foods, stereo equipment, body shops, vibrators. We have yoga, massage, body building and martial arts.

THE SELF-DIRECTED PLEASURE BUSINESS HAS BECOME AN AMERICAN OBSESSION.

We have gurus, swamis and personal trainers. We have personal development and self-growth. Girl Scout Troops runs off twice a week to have consciousness raising episodes at the junior high school. Huge sums of money are involved. We spend more than $250,000,000—a quarter of a billion dollars annually—for the rolling papers and more than six billion for weed. Four hundred million dollars are spent on jogging paraphernalia.

The self-indulgent, self-improvement pleasure industry—entertainment, travel, recreation, sensual stimulation, aesthetics, style and fashion—is the largest business in America. The business of Uncle Sam has become self-actualized pleasure.

Self-directed hedonic engineering drives the dom-species.

Before the 1960s, the orthodox hive philosophy insisted that "for every little pleasure there's pain, pain, pain." God was considered a beady-eyed accountant up there in Hive-Heaven keeping your hedonic balance in order. And woe be it to you if you overdrew on your pleasure account! Because the wages of fun were death—as every Hollywood movie warned.

The dom-species has come a long way from that prudishness, due in some part, to our friends from the Oriental philosophy department. We have learned that pleasure is not bound by some Newtonian conservation-of-energy-principle and thus balanced by pain. We understand that beauty is something that can be understood, can be learned, can be engineered. Pleasure is not an ejaculation reflex. It is an art, a science, a

BEAUTY IS SOMETHING THAT CAN BE UNDERSTOOD, CAN BE LEARNED, CAN BE ENGINEERED.

skilled performance, like playing the concert piano. It is something that can be studied and, through disciplined intelligence, increased. And, indeed, the more you do it, the better you get at it. Thus pleasure and intelligent hedonism are like tennis. Find someone who plays as well or better than yourself.

The neurosomatic rebirth, the Body Resurrection which occurred in the sexual revolution is an accomplished fact.

The Body has been uncovered. We're never going to return to prudish robot-hood.

The other aspect of the contelligence movement of the 1960s—the neurological revolution—was the discovery of the brain itself. A hundred years ago there was a taboo organ in Victorian England and in Freudian Vienna. Genitals were considered the unmentionable. Look at any newsstand and you will see that the genitals are no longer the unmentionables, but rather the unavoidables. Now the taboo organ, the organ that we cannot talk about or study intelligently is the brain. The next taboo is DNA actualization.

It is only since the development of neurology that science has begun to face the real meaning of the brain. The Brain is emerging from the closet. And it is scary, my friends!

It is frightening to every static, comfortable social and philosophic hive-notion to realize that you are carrying around behind your forehead a 100 billion-cell bioelectric computer that creates realities.

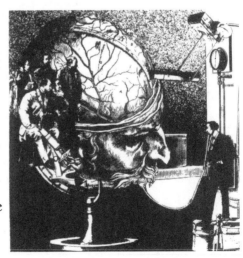

Through imprinting and reimprinting, the brain imposes the reality you inhabit. Everything you think and feel and sense and remember and learn is simply a process of brain functioning.

When a species understands that the brain is a tool, then it starts to think about directing and understanding this incredible instrument. And it begins using it to ask such embarrassing questions as—who designed the brain? And what is it for? And how do we use the brain?

I created a mutation signal called *Exo-Psychology: A Manual on the Use of the Human Brain According to the Instructions of the Manufacturers.* The title is a way of reminding us that the great realization of the 1960s was that

YOUR BRAIN CREATES YOUR OWN REALITY.

8

INTELLIGENCE
COUNTER-INTELLIGENCE

STUDYING COUNTERINTELLIGENCE is one way
to understand how intelligence can
be lowered. Counter-intelligence
incessantly seeks old facts about
other hives. Counter-intelligence continuously
searches for maps, blueprints, plans about intra-hive
activity—in spite of the fact that nothing of genetic
importance occurs within hives. Counter-intelligence
feverishly construct apparatuses, devices, networks
to limit our intelligence. Counter-intelligence bureaucracies, which includes the CIA, Senate investigating committees, and the old Soviet KGB lower
intelligence and makes us more stupid with time
tested techniques.

SECRECY

ANYONE WHO KEEPS SECRETS FROM YOU is your Essence
Enemy—acting to lower your most precious asset—
your intelligence. If intelligence is the ultimate good
then secrecy is the ultimate crime. Censorship is the
imposition of secrets.

COUNTER-INTELLIGENCE MAKES US STUPID

Disinformation

FALSE FACTS OBVIOUSLY INCREASE STUPIDITY. When Richard Helms lied under oath about CIA involvement in Chile, he was acting to keep the Senate and the American people stupid. When Dick Gregory and Mark Lane invent Kennedy conspiracy facts they are lowering the National Intelligence Index.

Secrecy is the most obvious and blatant technique for inhibiting intelligence and always designed to increase stupidity.

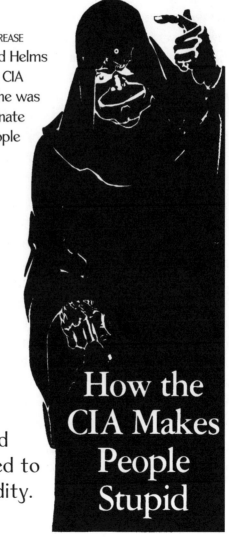

How the CIA Makes People Stupid

Sexual or Financial Immorality

A CLASSIC PLOY BY WHICH THE HIVE STIMULATES STUPIDITY is the
Immorality Placebo—usually sexual or financial.
First, the gene-pool sets up a Moral Taboo. Moral
Taboos are magnificent Intelligence Qualification
(IQ) devices because they get everyone in the hive
hung up on virtue-sin. The Moral Taboo must interfere with some normal, natural caste-behavior. It
must perversely prevent some castes from getting
something that they neurologically are wired to
want. Once brought
into focus by prescrip-
tion the Taboo be-
comes charged with
artificial cop-sinner
magnetism.

**IF THEY CAN GET
YOU ASKING THE
WRONG QUESTIONS,
THEY DON'T HAVE
TO WORRY ABOUT
ANSWERS.**

—PYNCHON

Genesis, the first
chapter in the Judeo-
Christian Bible, clearly
sets out the strategy of the Immorality Placebo—
using good versus evil as a fascinating distraction, a
front, a ploy. There are two forbidden trees in the
Garden of Eden. The serpent—now exposed as agent
provocateur—gets Eve and Adam to eat the fruit of
the first tree, which provides the Knowledge—
substitute the word "hang-up"—of Good and Evil,
thus forgetting about the second tree, which bears
the fruit of self-actualization and immortality.

Interestingly, the Immorality Placebo has been
formalized by Pynchon as one of his *"Proverbs for
Paranoids—If they can get you asking the wrong
questions, they don't have to worry about answers."*

THREE FUNCTIONS
OF INTELLIGENCE

WHEN THE EVOLUTIONARY AGENT GI GURDJIEFF was a young
cub in the Caucasian Alps, he suffered a minor wound
in a scuffle with a chum. It seems that Gurdjieff criti-
cized the sound of the chum's flatulence. In the boyish
roughhouse that followed Gurdjieffs tooth was loos-
ened. When he reached in his mouth, the tooth came
away in his fingers. Examining the technological relic
he noticed that it had seven roots. And each root had
a drop of brilliantly crimsoned blood.

When his companions showed no interest in this
unusual phenomenon, the Young Agent ran to the
village dentist, who examined the specimen with
interest. *"Amazing,"* said the Dentist, handing the tooth
back to Gurdjieff, *"I've never seen anything like it in the
fifty years I have been extracting teeth. I don't understand it. It's a real mystery."*

"But what does it mean?" asked youth Gurdjieff..
The Dentist shrugged.

"But what shall we do about it?" persisted the
Young Gurdjieff. The Dentist shrugged again. *"Consider
yourself lucky that it came out that easily. You've saved
yourself three rubles."*

The young Gurdjieff resolved on the spot that for
the rest of his life he would do nothing but study
those events which the rest of the human race ignored
as mysterious. Evolutionary Agent, Pynchon dealt with
the same problem at a time when The mysterious and
inexplicable was dominating the foreign policy of every
terrestrial country. *"Anti-paranoia,"* said Pynchon, *"is
that eerie thought that nothing is connected to anything."*

Second Intelligence Principle

GURDJIEFF WAS GIVEN GOOD ADVICE BY HIS GRANDMOTHER when he was a young man in the Armenian area of the Black Sea which he followed. His grandmother was dying. Over two hundred relatives came to see her in her home—including scores of great-grandchildren. The mob of relatives filled the corridors and patios of the house with their lamenting. But the Grandmother would see no one except her oldest friend, a German doctor named Wimpe.

After many hours Doctor Wimpe emerged from the dying woman's room. The crowd, expecting an announcement of death was surprised when the doctor said that Grandmother wished to talk to only one of her many relatives. Little Georgie (Giorgione) as Gurdjieff was called.

The young Gurdjieff approached the aged woman and stood respectfully by the side of her bed. She motioned him closer, grasped his hand lightly, looked intently into his eyes. She gave a satisfied nod and motioned him even closer.

"*Listen,*" she said, "*you are the only one who will understand. Boy, swear to me that you will never forget what I tell you?*"

"*I shall never forget, Grandmother,*" swore Gurdjieff.

"*Never do anything that anyone else does. Never think what anyone else thinks. And, most important, trust no one's maps but your own. And trust your own maps only for the moment,*" the old woman said emphatically.

Third Intelligence Principle

THE THIRD PRINCIPLE that Gurdjieff used to guide his life and to increase his intelligence was passed on to him by an illiterate peasant. Every year after the harvest this peasant walked to Moscow to purchase items unavailable in the village, drink some vodka and see the city sights. As was his habit, after the peasant conducted his business he relaxed in an outdoor cafe drinking vodka and listened to music. But this time he suddenly remembered that he had forgotten to purchase a special book that his oldest son had requested. So the peasant and a tipsy friend set off to find a book store.

The book was found. "*That will be 13 rubles,*" said the clerk.

"*But the price printed on the cover is 10 rubles,*" protested the peasant.

"*The extra three are for the postage,*" replied the clerk.

"*Splendid,*" said the peasant handling the clerk fifteen rubles.

The clerk returned with the change, courteous salutations were exchanged and the peasant left the store. As the two peasants continued their walk down the boulevard the friend inquired with impatience, *"Dmitri, why did you pay three rubles too much and why do you feel so merry about being overcharged?"*

The peasant laughed loudly. *"When we're on a spree in Moscow, we pay the whole tab, including the postage."*

UNCERTAINTY PRINCIPLE

One OF THE MOST IMPORTANT FORCES in moving human intelligence from the old science—Euclidian-Newtonian—to the new science—Einsteinian-Planck—is the Principle of Uncertainty introduced by Werner Heisenberg, which states that the very presence of experimenters and their measuring instruments becomes a determining factor in the field of investigation. Any hope of objectivity seemed to be eliminated. A philosophic angst, a sense of scientific futility, was the first reaction to Heisenberg's dictum. *"Alas,"* the Newtonians groaned, *"we can never really know what God or Nature hath wrought, because the very act of investigating changes the situation."*

Actually Heisenberg's Principle is one of self-actualized determinacy.

Everything we see and know is a function of our reality-mapping—a function of the way we program our brains. This is the Principle of Neurological Determinacy. With the self-confidence, courage and freedom thus attained, we can accept the responsibility implied. Within the limits of our genetic stage we can responsibly determine—construct, create, fabricate—the new realities we inhabit!

EINSTEIN-ESFANDIARY INTELLIGENCE TEST

IN 1944, Einstein designed and took his own intelligence test. Later, it was revise by F.M. Esfandiary, who thus increased his own intelligence—I^2. The first item on the Einstein-Esfandiary Intelligence Test (Standard Alien Intelligence Test item) asked, *"How do you define intelligence?"* Einstein answered that the way one defines intelligence is the most important step taken in life.

Intelligence—like the nerve cells upon which it is based—has three functions—reception, mapping and performance.

FUNCTIONS OF INTELLIGENCE

Reception is the ability to expand—direct the scope, source, intensity of information received. This is consciousness expansion—opening up to new data.

Mapping is the ability to joyously revise your metaphors of reality in response to new information—including other people's metaphors.

Performance is the ability to construct external-communication apparati, in fusion with others, which stimulate expanded information-input, new maps-of-reality and improved networks.

The function of evolution is to stimulate an Increase in Intelligence — I^2. An evolutionary action is one designed to increase your intelligence. An Evolutionary Agent is one who continually works to expand input of information, revise reality metaphors and raise the intelligence of self and others.

THE ONLY SMART THING TO DO IS TO GET SMARTER.

The second item on the Einstein-Esfandiary test asked, "*Can intelligence be increased?* Yes! Intelligence can be increased. Our brains are designed to increase our intelligence. The aim and strategy of evolution is to raise the intelligence of species. The development of every individual from infancy to maturity is the story of Intelligence Increase—I^2. The only smart thing to do is to get smarter.

HOW TO INCREASE INTELLIGENCE

ALEISTER CROWLEY TAUGHT US that there are three ways to increase your intelligence:

First, continually expand the scope, source, and intensity of the information you receive.

Second, constantly revise your reality maps and seek new metaphors about the future to understand what's happening now.

Third, develop external networks for increasing intelligence. In particular, spend all your time with people as smart or smarter than you.

9

WAR INCREASES INTELLIGENCE

THE FACT THAT AMERICAN PSYCHOLOGY after 1946 was an offspring of military psychology is neither alarming nor unexpected. Throughout human history the Warrior Caste has introduced each new technology—mechanical, medical, social, and even bureaucratic.

The military serves hive-terrestrials as the pioneer avant garde. Most intelligence structures are originated by their military who function as suspicious antennae for their societies. They are charged with the responsibility for finding out what's happening over there in the next hive; for sniffing out what the territorial rivals are doing, and for protecting the hive.

The Warrior Caste—the warrior insects—are genetically wired to act as paranoid sense-organs for the body-social.

As Thomas Pynchon pointed out in his book *Gravity's Rainbow*, wars—however cruel and pointless they may seem to liberals—are necessary competitions to stimulate technological advances. Inter-hive conflicts are evolutionary devices to make Earthlings move faster, see farther, communicate better, transport, organize and heal ourselves more effectively. For an extended discussion of the genetic meaning of war in species evolution, refer to my book, *Neuropolitics: The Sociobiology of Human Metamorphosis.*

After the new technology has been tested and proved by the Warrior Caste, it is then co-opted by the other techno-castes who convert the new energy into hive use. The order in which castes take over a new energy is fixed—Political Power Caste, Engineer Commercial Caste, Moral Domesticator Caste. In advanced societies, which have met these security satisfaction challenges, the technology is then co-opted by post-hive individual castes—Artist Caste, Neurologician Caste, Neurogeneticist Caste.

The history of preflight civilization is this cycle of technological evolution. Each caste is robot-wired to use the new technology and harness it to the specialized caste function. Pynchon outlines how this new technology—psychology—was initiated during wartime by the requirements of the military and how mind-control techniques have been taken over by the Managerial, Technician-Intellectual and Social-Moral Castes. *Gravity's Rainbow,* of course, was a powerful signal from the Artistic Caste—the change agents. The book is a brilliant attempt to use psychological knowledge to free individuals from the limiting past.

Without understanding all the implications, the military during World War II mobilized enormous national resources to create new technologies. These included air-transportation, electronic communication, nuclear energy, production of labor-saving gadgets, and psychological assessment of personality. All of these breakthroughs were produced by the patriotic emergency. Uncle Sam, the national self-indulgent consumer, wanted—and he got it! He demanded, "Gimme 50,000 bombers"— and the hive gladly produced! "Gimme a radar system that will detect metal miles-high-in-the-sky" and he got it! Sam said, "Gimme ships and planes so I can ship ten million lusty young warriors in two years to the five continents" and he got it!

NEUROLOGICAL IMPLICATIONS

THE NEUROGENETIC IMPLICATIONS ARE STAGGERING. The American gene pool sprayed sperm from 20 million testicles around the globe—the fastest, largest genetic experiment in planet history. The so-called "war effort" performing the genetic function of mixing up sperm-egg exchanges in addition to the cultural interactions—the new imprint models imposed on youthful nervous systems of both the invaders and the invaded. When American G.I.'s rode into German towns astride sleek-powerful military machines an irreversible impression was made upon the impressionable German minds.

The American gene pool sprayed
sperm from 20 million testicles around
the globe—the fastest, largest genetic
experiment in planet history.

In the context of this all-out hive-war solidarity it
was considered an honor for physicists like Einstein
and Fermi to make bombs, and for psychologists
like B.F. Skinner and Harry Murray to offer their
services to do secret work for the OSS-CIA.

INNER AND OUTER SPACE

DURING WORLD WAR II Hitler was approached by a
committee of distinguished scientists from the Max
Planck Institute and the Prague Pharmaceutical
Laboratories, who proposed the theory that the
earth is hollow. Und zo, if we can find the entrance
or punch a hole through to the interior, mein Gott,
all sorts of new military adventures suggest themselves. We can pop up behind enemy lines and
conquer the external surface. Who controls the
inner surface of a sphere controls the outer world.
Heil Hitler! *Heute Deutschland; Morgen das Inner-
welt, morgen morgen das Extra-welt.*

This legend has been passed on, in print, by
anti-Nazi agents to demonstrate the insanity of
Hitler. There is no hard data concerning whether
der Feuhrer really did divert scientific energy—
which could have supported atomic bomb-research
or improved rocket-research—into inner-earth
exploration. But let us assume that the legend is
true, that Adolph did believe in an "inner-world" and
did, indeed, initiate scientific inner-world-explora-

tion. To make this assumption is to credit Hitler with considerable—if twisted—prophetic genius. Inner-world aspirations in 1935 clearly anticipated the Neurological Revolution of the 1960s, which sent over one hundred million Americans digging in psychic mole-holes, pursuing the vision of an inner-world rebirth. Heil, Werner Erhard.

Who controls the inner surface of a sphere controls the outer world. Heil Hitler!

Hitler, like many premature evolutes, inhabited a post-terrestrial set of realities. Total power in the context of Tibetan Buddhism obviously activated the self-indulgent and the self-actualized circuits in his nervous system. Hitler, however, made the same error that millions of naive trippers made in the 1960s. He failed to understand that the very self-centered, post-hive consciousness that exhilarated him to messianic perception was also available to others. He was not informed that the self-actualized brain must include in its mapping the reality that other self-actualized, futique brains exist and are independently building neighboring future plan-its.

SELF-ACTUALIZATION

SELF-ACTUALIZATION is a post-hive, post-terrestrial tool. Black Magic is the use of futique knowledge to gain control over the passed-present. Hitler was evilly using post-terrestrial tools to grab terrestrial power. It is considered genetic wickedness to use post-hive knowledge to control the old hive. Futique

ANYTHING THAT DESTROYS BUREAUCRACY ENHANCES EVOLUTION. competence is a sacred trust—to be used to propel the hive-mythos into a new ecological niche. Zionists commit the same genetic crime when they use advanced technology to go back and conquer the primitive Arabs. By 1976 the rumor spread that this Hitler myth was invented by Zionist Evolutionary Agents who had participated in the CIA's LSD experiments.

Hitler's vision of living inside rather than on the surface of a satellite-planet is, of course, a most accurate forecast of subsequent stages of evolution. The ecological niche to which post-humans are now moving involves hollow mini-world plan-its constructed in space beyond the planet's gravitational pull.

Throughout the range of evolution those who migrate within capsules of their own construction are more advanced than those who live clinging to the outside of capsules someone else built.

The problem with military technology is, of course, that wars end. But terrestrial bureaucracies persevere, particularly those of the winning side. The reason postwar losers, like Germany and Japan, rebounded more rapidly than the winners—England, France, Russia—was that the bureaucracies of the losers were destroyed. Anything that destroys a bureaucracy enhances evolution.

The release of atomic energy was a mutational moment....

After World War II, the massive industries which had been geared to produce war tools were converted to civilian goods. The managers and technical boys were ready to convert the assembly lines from tanks to fin-tailed cars. The radar factories were converted to television manufacture. America, during the 1950s, went on the biggest materialism consumer spree in history.

HIVE-ADJUSTMENT

THE WARTIME PSYCHOLOGICAL TECHNOLOGY was also converted to civilian consumption. Person- ality assessment techniques were taken over by the managerial powers and used to select and train employees. A new, gigantic industry emerged employing clinical psychologists and coun- selors and a new social-moral concept of human nature—adjustment.

Those who matured during the self-discovery 1960s and the self-actualized 1970s did not know that the aim of personality-clinical psychology and psychiatry during the 50s was hive-adjustment. Not surprising, really, when we recall that the Firm started it all in the 1940s "Their" aim was, we recall, the preservation of the past, the prevention of change. To understand the gravity of the situation, remember: There was no concept of personal change in the 1950s. Human personality was seen as a fixed quality, which could and should be adjusted to the system. Old-style psychiatrists—formerly called alienists—guarded the psychotic. The radical wing, psychoanalysis, taught that after five years of intensive treatment, five hours a week, the patient might get enough insight to wearily adjust and to discuss his neurosis at cocktail parties.

ANYONE BORN AFTER 1945 IS A MUTANT

NOW LET'S FINE-TUNE THE TIME MACHINE and focus on what has happened since 1945. We're all so involved that we may not appreciate the incredible changes of the last half of the 20th Century. We choose the year 1945 for obvious reasons; that was when our species fissioned nuclear structure thoughtfully at Alamogordo and blindly at Nagasaki and Hiroshima. The release of atomic energy is a mutational moment in the history of every nursery planet.

It's useful to assume that in 1945 every living organism of every species, on this planet, picked up this fallout and radiation message and transmitted it through their nervous system to RNA and back to DNA: "Hey, the domesticated primates are fissioning the atom! It's time to leave the planet because nuclear energies are not supposed to be used on a tiny, shrinking planet like ours." At this moment an astounding acceleration of intelligence occurred! *Review the evidence.*

The best evolutionary stages to inhabit are those of intense, dramatic inner-outer exploration—like 1960-1980.

Since 1945 we have fissioned and fusioned the atom. Decoding the DNA Code allowed us, at that moment in history, to confront the possibility of genetic engineering, cloning, and biological immortality. Since 1945, medical science has eliminated, one by one, most of the scourges and plagues which have terrorized our species since the beginning of re-corded history

Television

ONE OF THE MOST IMPORTANT THINGS TO HAPPEN to the new species born after 1945 is neuroelectronic consum-erism—Television. Every American child born after 1945 crawled out of the crib, toddled across the room, and with tiny, chubby, baby hands reached the boob tube and began dialing and tuning realities. Wheaties, no! Post Toasties? Maybe. Coke? Maybe. 7-Up, Ford, Carter, Chevrolet, Ford, Carter,

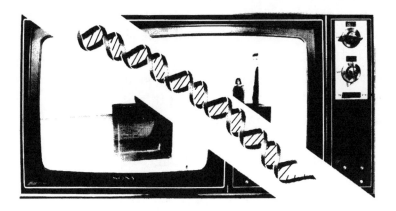

Disneyland, Disneyland, Disneyland, Disneyland. Children learned how to be reality consumers, watchers of reality commercials, selectors of reality products, actively dialing a wide frequency spectrum of passive receptivity. Eventually TV programmer got the message and rolled out one Reality Program after another and the public lapped it up.

The Sun Belt kid born after 1945 experiences more realities in one week than the most affluent aristocrats of the past experienced in a lifetime.

GENETIC TRAITORS

ONLY SIX TIMES IN THE 10,000 YEARS preceding the 1920s did a paedomorphic rejection of terminal adulthood by the juveniles of the species occur. This means that thirteen times in 2Y2 billion years one generation was called upon to assume the most difficult responsibility assigned to any individual nervous system. The role of genetic traitor emerged—active resistance to the monolithic pressure of adult domestication, a dramatic break with hive culture, escape from the very gene pool that gives continuity and safety to individuals.

Neoteny requires inconceivable strength. The species, at the peak of its strength and specialized survival skill, and crazed by the sense that it has peaked, throws all of its resources against the youthful traitors. A genetic intelligence test results. Attempting to thwart the mutation, the species hurls its moral sanctions, its scorn, its police forces, it's wily, canny old tricks at the mutating juveniles.

The species attempts to check, test and challenge the upstart renegades.

If the paedomorphic rebels appear too soon, or in the wrong place—not on the Western Frontier—then they are easily crushed. The kids don't make any headway east of La Brea—too bad if they appear in Madrid or Athens or Jerusalem or Moscow. Only when the genetic hour has struck and only on the changeable Western rim can neoteny or the rejection of terminal adulthood succeed.

In the decade 1964-1974 a small handful—less than 100,000—juveniles performed this extraordinary genetic feat. Using the available electronic communication technology they formed a global network and sent out the signal—*Drop Out.*

The adult fury unleashed upon this small band of Evolutionary Agents was savage and brutal. The pressures were incalculable. The visible leaders were singled out for particular attack by the adult authority and the casualty rate was tragically high. Janis Joplin. Jimmy Hendrix. Jim Morrison. James Dean. Elvis Presley paid the ultimate price.

Young Evolutionary Agents, however brutal the treatment they received from the hive authorities, were linked together in an unspoken peer-network. They were all together in rejecting adult authority. In spite of the scorn heaped on "hippies" they all shared a moral superiority to their parents. This gene pool was committed to change and didn't offer the solidity of the traditional parent-hive.

10

SPINNING UP
THE GENETIC HIGHWAY

O N EVERY BIOLOGICAL WOMB-PLANET the Genetic Highway climbs from East to West in the temperate zones. These are easily located in terms of spherical geometry where the 30th to 45th degrees latitude—North and South—locate the runways along which gene pools accelerate to Escape Velocity.

North-South is an astro-neurological constant based on magnetic charge. East-West is thus an astro-neurological constant based on spin. On every womb-planet in the galaxy rotational orientation relative to the home star determines the direction of migrating intelligence.

North-South is charge.
East-West is spin.

> ## EXPERIENCE THE POWER OF SPIN
>
> IMAGINE THAT YOU STAND FIFTY MILES—250,000 feet—high. Face West and sense the earth-spin moving you backwards. You would have to keep striding forward one thousand miles an hour to keep the sun at the same angle. This would be an easy stroll—one hundred paces an hour would do it.
>
> Next, face East and feel that you are falling downward, pushed by spin-momentum. You are falling towards the sun, which will rise in front of you, below you. You are moving downward at one thousand miles an hour.

Primitive organisms face the sun, to ride passively towards the sun. More advanced organisms develop the mobility necessary to chase the sun, to move against the rotational tide.

The navigational rule is simple. When you greet the sun, after the night, you are facing the East. You are facing Asia. The word Asia comes from Greek-Latin, "region of the rising sun." The name Europe comes from Greek and Sematic, "land of the setting sun."

EAST IS PAST

WHEN YOU FACE EAST you are peering down into the past. Our gene pools came from the East. When you see the sun disappear over the horizon you are looking up into the future. This basic attitudinal orientation on womb-planets is based upon spin-momentum.

Spin is a fundamental defining characteristic of energy-matter.

WHEN YOU MOVE EAST you are being carried down the spin-axis. You are riding the globe, moving with the rotational inertia. When you move West, you climb up against the rotation. Spin is one of the fundamental defining characteristics of energy-matter.

In "Fundamental Particles with Charm," published in *Scientific American,* Roy F. Schwitters wrote, "At the level of elementary particles the properties of matter are remarkably few. A particle can have mass or energy, and it can have momentum, including the intrinsic angular momentum called *spin.*"

SPIN IS FUNDAMENTAL

SPIN IS A FUNDAMENTAL PERSONALITY CHARACTERISTIC of all energy structures, not only elementary particles. It is the wheeling of galaxies. The movements of humans living on a spinning globe. Spinning is the orientation of all living organisms to the rotational momentum of the womb-planets or designed plan-its.

WHAT IS SO ABOVE IS SO BELOW. The Hermetic Doctrine holds that, what is so above is so below. Recapitulation theory holds that the same sequences re-evolve at all levels of energy. Neurologic thus leads us to expect spin to be a basic dimension of biological structure.

Spin-caste is as fundamental a determinant of human behavior as sexual caste. Spin is as basic to life as sex. To understand terrestrial humans it is as necessary to understand their spin-castes as it is to identify their sexual castes.

There is fore-spin—brains geared to move west into the future. There is backspin—brains wired to face the past.

Spin-caste is determined by how far West you and your gene pool have migrated—and at what speed. Fore-spin is moving West, facing the momentum. Pushing up against the rotation to develop mobility and attain altitude. It is moving into the future, ascending into the empty ecological niches.

The empty New American Continents—lobes— were discovered and filled from Europe, not from Asia. The wisdom of the East sailed across the Pacific. California was explored and settled from

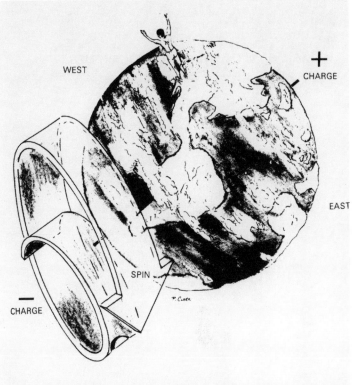

SPIN IS AS BASIC TO LIFE AS SEX. Europe. Venice was not discovered by wandering Chinese. Asians did not colonize Europe. Where were the Chinese Drakes and Vasco da Gamas? Throughout history, even today, when Asians come West, they use western modes of transportation. How come? Eastern countries compress into xenophobic centralized anthills, discouraging migration. It is because of backspin.

Backspin is sitting, immobile, with your back to momentum. Oriental-orientation is passively riding the down-wave. Occidental-orientation is actively pushing against rotation, continually being tested, shaped, formed by the airflow, your antennae continually probing forward for the next pathway opening up.

BASIC POETIC-MYSTIC POLARITIES

East	West
Earth	Heaven
Passive	Active
Piety	Intelligence
Past	Future
Simplicity	Complexity
Tradition	Change
Control	Freedom
Unity	Diversity
Stasis	Mobility

Only from an Einsteinian, relativistic post-terrestrial attitude can one realize that East-West means down-up. Liberation from Newtonian geography and recognition of geo-relativity are necessary stages of evolution. How do you determine down-up on a spinning sphere? Against the spin is up.

EAST-WEST MEANS DOWN-UP

THE MOST INSTRUCTIVE WAY TO LOOK AT A WORLD-MAP is to reposition the map so that East is down. Then reexperience the long climb of humanity from East to West. The busy caravans like ant-flies shuttling up and down the Asian trade routes. The enormous ant-armies of Alexander overrunning the past—no worlds for him to conquer westward. Genghis Khan's fast-moving mobile, equine technology storming upward. The explosion of Muslim columns.

WHY DIDN'T WANDERING CHINESE DISCOVER VENICE?

Roman legions painfully pushing up into Gaul sense the movement of human swarms over the centuries—the empire-hives sending out columns and waves, the exploratory probes westward. The flotillas of frail craft moving up the Atlantic, shipping that most basic cargo: sperm and eggs. The other cargoes are support-logistic.

When you watch the sun disappear over the horizon you are looking into the future.

The greatest technological problem faced by DNA on this planet was scaling the Atlantic Ocean. For over a thousand years, from 40 to 1400 AD, the waves of mobile-elite sperm-eggs splashed up to the Western-European Atlantic beach-ledges—and waited. It was the greatest swarming phenomenon in human history! Port-cities teeming with migragents, explorers, and space-travelers. Western Fever! Peerers into the unknown. Pourers over maps of future lands. Migrating gene pools freaking out for new spaces. Kings and Queens caught by the fever. And Columbus—Columbus obsessed with this Everest problem, commanded by genetic directive to scale this mountain of water three-thousand-miles-high. He said, "I gave the keys of those mighty barriers of ocean which were closed with such mighty chains."

ATLANTIC ASCENT

NOTE THE TIMING OF ATLANTIC ASCENT. It had to await the Protestant Reformation. The Luther self-actualization freed gene pools from the Catholic-hive center. Only a society of self-actualized families, democratically linked together, was capable of pushing gene pools three-thousand-miles up, into the storm altitudes of the North Atlantic.

Recall that the ascent had been made over and over again during the ten centuries before Columbus by doughty Vikings, fervent Irish monks and hundreds of masculine bands. Some returned to tell the story of the new ecological niche. But the signal did not activate the swarm because the technology for lifting gene pools three-thousand-miles into the unknown had not yet emerged. Thousands of European sailors who found the new lands did not return. Instead, they were absorbed by native gene pools. If thousands of Amazon female sailors had reached North America before the Protestant Revolution, they too would have been swallowed up by the native gene pools.

It always requires a technical breakthrough to move sperm-egg colonies to a higher altitude—a higher velocity.

Sperm-Egg Colonies

A GENE POOL IS A SPECIES-UNIT capable of protecting its young over several generations. Marauding bands of astronauts, like Francis Drake and John Wayne, are a beginning probe. But nothing happens until the family-units move together. You see, the King-Emperor does not want to migrate. He does not want to leave the seat of Imperial power and luxury. The feudal society cannot migrate, which is likely why Catholic countries couldn't pull it off. The Holders of the Land have to stay on the land. Feudal Catholic-Monarchies are flashy in the first stage of opening-up of a new ecological niche. The second-

born sons, the Dukes' younger brothers, sail off with
crack-troops to establish secure footholds. It was
genetic folly for Spaniards to mate with Paleolith
natives. None the less permanent military settle-
ments have to breed with the natives and the mes-
tizo result is uniformly disastrous because the
second-string, invasive male-warriors mate down
with intellectually unrealized conquered females.

A gene pool is a species-unit capable
of protecting its young over several
generations.

11

MOBILITY IS NOBILITY

THERE IS AN IMMUTABLE LAW OF NEURO-GEOG-
RAPHY which governs terrestrial
politics—the evolution of intelligence
moves East to West. When you go back
East—note the retrograde terminology—you are
going back in time, down in intelligence and lower
in evolution.

Let me restate it simply: Westerners are signifi-
cantly smarter, freer, more creative, more future-
oriented than Easterners. Easterners operate at
lower forms of evolution. Easterners, it is true, are
more specialized—but, as we have learned from
dinosaurs, specialization means Terminal Adulthood. Civilizations are, by definition, adult—i.e. passe.

**Specialization
means terminal
adulthood.**

Freedom moves from East to West

WESTERN GENE-POOLS ARE ALWAYS FREER, more adolescent, more mobile than Eastern gene-pools. In the Genetic Breeding Book, mobility is nobility.

The most intelligent and the freest people on the planet have been propelled by their gene pools to the Western belt of this continent—Arizona, Texas, California, Oregon, Washington—the ecological niche of the future. Each Westerner is the hopeful adolescent blossom of the old Eastern roots.

When you move back East from the Pacific—be on guard. You are moving down into primitive, inflexible, cynical terrain. Chicago is a tough, mammalian jungle compared to San Diego. New England is a monument to the static past. Easterners, in their neolithic shrewdness are skillful, political mammals. They are adepts in Newtonian competitions. Do not try to hustle Easterners on their own turf. New York is the center of money power, Washington is the center of barnyard political force, and Boston the capital of antiquated Puritan culture—but there is no freedom, no spirit of growth and development, no enthusiasm for change in the Adult Eastern Hive.

NEVER TRY TO HUSTLE EASTERNERS ON THEIR OWN TURF.

These remarks are in no way chauvinistic. All Westerners are migrated Easterners! I was born at West Point, New York and teenaged in Massachusetts. I honor my damp roots and respect their venerable, unchanging traditions. I thank the New England educational system for activating my migration button.

It is no accident that all the laws which restrict youthful freedom come from grim, prudish Eastern hives.

We must be aware of the natural tendency of Eastern hive leaders to frighten stay-put yokels with stories of Western instability. Sure Californians and Arizonians and Texans are diverse, flamboyant, juvenile and easy to deride. It's always that way. Frontier regions encourage the formation of new gene-pools, wide-open territories that allow cultural experimentation and future fabrication are always easy to ridicule from the docile, adult, traditional bunkers of the Orient.

The age-old Chinese think that all Occidentals are crazy kids because we believe in individual reality and personal change. To the old Soviets individualism is hooliganism! We grant that an Easterner, in the secure cocoon of adult conformity and centralized dogmatic **MOBILITY IS NOBILITY.** repetition, is shocked by the insane insistence of Westerners to "be themselves." We grant that the individual or small cult is kooky-vulnerable in contrast to the monolithic stability of specialized gene-pools which repeat what their parents did and cling to the myths of their grandparents. The independent Western pioneer is easily ridiculed. But the fact remains—freedom to experiment, courage to change, energy to recreated is always a Westward High.

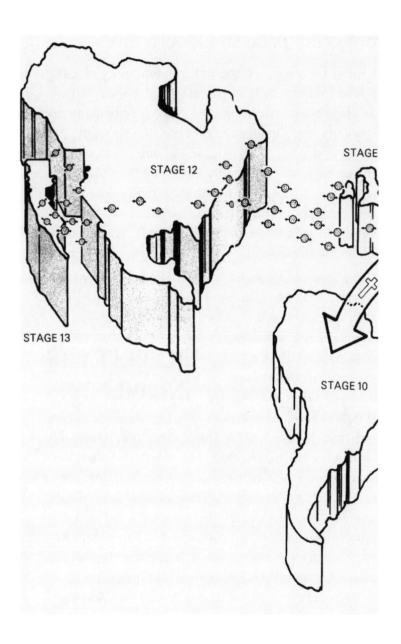

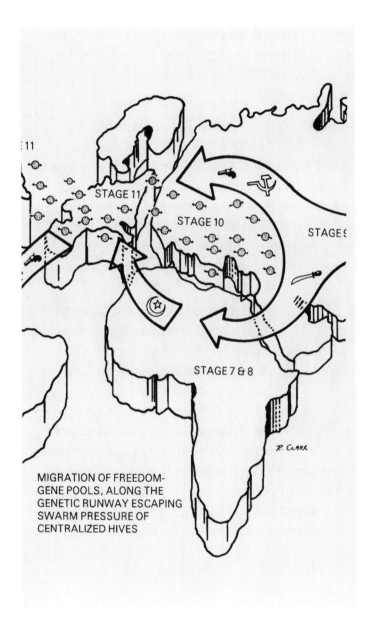

MIGRATION OF FREEDOM-
GENE POOLS, ALONG THE
GENETIC RUNWAY ESCAPING
SWARM PRESSURE OF
CENTRALIZED HIVES

GENETIC INTELLIGENCE

GENETIC INTELLIGENCE IS MEASURED by the ability to move gene pools upward, angling always westward, pushing against, always being shaped by, reformed by, activated by, mutated by spin-pressure from *The Future*

The truth of the Occidental Ascendance becomes comically clear when we move down and back East across the Atlantic Ocean. The Greenwich time zones are in centuries. If Boston is two hundred years before Los Angeles—no accident that the current Neurological Capital of the planet has been given the high-altitude title "City of the Angels", then surely we see that London is four hundred years back and down.

What, in truth, can we expect from England? Elizabethan Style? Repetitious tradition? Culture? Only in the sense of a class structure which penalizes new genetic intelligence' in favor of inherited privilege. Parent-child inheritance of bureaucratic advantage always drives the superior-futique genes into migration. This is not a political complaint, but a neurogenetic I.Q. test. The genetically active, whether descended from the sperm-ova of prince or pauper—every gene-pool contains its princes and paupers, always migrate West. Those who rely on power remain in the Eastern capital.

If England is a comic opera
what can we say about France?

Paris is a museum of dusty Louis XIV grandeur. And what, in relevant charity for the past, can be said about the lessons that an intelligent terrestrial primate can learn today in Lisbon? Madrid? Rome? Athens? Cairo? Beirut? Jerusalem?

There is this to be said for NATO nations. They are the most Western—the freest and smartest gene-pools of the Old Continent. Examine a map of the Euro-Asian land mass. Color in blue those countries which are democratic, which respect human rights, which outlaw torture, which allow any cultural or individual experimentation. You will see that the blue countries cluster nervously at the Western borders of the huge, Euro-Asian hemisphere. Notice as you go East you find more government restrictions, more centralization, more contempt for the individual, more commitment to tradition and familial-dictatorship.

TO LIVE EAST OF DENVER IS TO FAIL THE INTELLIGENCE TEST

One winter I traveled from San Diego to Buffalo and told the shivering natives, "Buffalo is an intelligence test you have failed. So you have to stay here and repeat Buffalo IA." Can there possibly be one intelligent person left in North Ireland? Uganda? Any Ugandan with more than eight billion neurons surely has swum a river or climbed a mountain to flee from that jungle of primitive barbarism.

Buffalo is an intelligence test
you have failed.

12

WESTWARD HIGH

The time has come to learn how to read the Occidental Altimeter. When you move East you crash-land in the past. Consider our liberal Potomac executives and congressional busybodies who continually ignore the wisdom of Washington's farewell advice not to meddle in the affairs of the Old World. Poor President Carter sent a senile envoy, Averell Harriman, to Cyprus to settle the quarrel between the Turks and the Greeks—forgetting that midbrain Mediterraneans have been fighting each other about mammalian territorial borders for 5,000 years!

Then came Secretary of State Vance attempting to mediate border disputes between the Palestinians and the Hebrews! How about that for a genetic laugh! And Nixon tilted in favor of Pakistan! And Kissinger intervened Lon Nol in Cambodian politics thus assuming the karma for two million dead and creating the ultimate insectoid state-postwar Cam-

bodia. Foreign policy is the game of mad monsters
playing chess blindfolded with mammalian-gene-
pools as pawns. Foreign policy is totally foreign to
the American Myth. That's why accented Europeans
like Kissinger and Brzezinski are selected to be
Secretaries of State. It's a European game several
centuries old.

Foreign policy is the game of mad monsters playing chess blindfolded....

Here's your American Ecological Foreign Policy. The
folks of the Old World inhabit pre-civilized, barbarian gene-pools. Europeans and Africans and Asians
are our own animal origins still obsessed with
territorial conflict. This is not said in disinterest. By
all means send food and veterinary medicines to the
Old World. By all means send the old gene-pools
invitations that freedom, change, mobility and
intelligence increase awaits in the West. But to
meddle in European-African-Asian politics is an
attempt to reconcile the ancient quarrel between
rabbits and foxes. Shall free Americans take sides in
back yard competition between the red ants and
the black ants of South Africa, or the ferocious-
fanatics of the Middle East?

Terrorists wanting to destroy technology and Western ways to take us back to the Old World originated where? In the Middle East—where else?

Interestingly enough, the national, tribal folk of Africa
say they just want to be left alone and have no

loyal commitments to Pentagon politicians. By all
means let them alone.

THE DARK AGES

AN INTERESTING THING HAPPENED when the caravans of
futique gene-pools fleeing West hit the beaches of the
North Atlantic. No place to go. The Dark Ages (sic)
occurred when this Westward wave of intelligent
gene-pools crashed against the North Atlantic wall.
Thousands of restless gene-pools had to wait in
Western Europe until they got smart enough—techno-
logically skillful enough—to move sperm-egg flotilla up
the North Atlantic. The vanguard elite clustered in
Ireland—as far West as possible. Darwinians didn't
understand. It's not survival of the fittest; it's the
evolution of the fastest in the Human Race.

COCOON PREPARATION
FOR MIGRATION

HERE WAS THE FAMILIAR TEST of nerve and intelligence. During
the Dark Ages the hive fear merchants said, "Stay put.
The world is flat. If you sail across the North Atlantic
you'll fall off the edge. You'll be eaten by dragons, or
busted by narcotic agents." Or whatever they spooked
people with back then.

Recall here the etymology of the world
locomotor. Fast movers throughout the
history of evolution have always been
considered "loco" or "crazy" by static hive-
establishments.

The Paleolithic conservatives warned restless marine creatures away from the shoreline. Unicellular bureaucrats warned protozoic out-castes about hooking up in multicellular linkages.

The explosion did take place. The world is not flat, it's a spinning sphere. Eventually the DNA code reacting to the stimuli of pollution and overpopulation activated the mobility-agents. Celtic Rangers were the first to climb the Atlantic. Prince Henry, the Navigator, sent Vasco da Gama around the Horn; Queen Isabella pawned her jewels to fund the NASA explorations of Christopher Columbus. Queen Elizabeth got an appropriation from Parliament to fund the astronaut voyages of Sir Francis Drake. At this swarming moment of expansion and exploration, the great European powers reached the high points of their culture, drama, poetry, art, science and philosophy.

IT'S NOT SURVIVAL OF THE FITTEST; IT'S THE EVOLUTION OF THE FASTEST IN THE HUMAN RACE.

That Dark Age was a pre-mutation period of growth-limitation, fear, bureaucratic hive-restriction, proto-Naderism which said: "Movement is unsafe at any speed."

COME JOIN THE PARTY

To say that Old World natives inhabit primitive ecological niches, is not to be chauvinistic. I descend from Irish stock. I look at Erin with an affectionate "roots" perspective and must admit that every intelligent Irishman and Irishwoman has long since migrated West! "Across the water." Can you believe that today in Belfast, Catholic kids are raised to murderously hate Protestants—and Protestants teach their youngsters to genocidally despise Papists. That's at least four hundred years in the past! And, at the current accelerated rate of evolution, Californians are as far removed from the Reformation Wars as Luther was from the Neanderthal.

Californians are as far removed from the Reformation Wars as Luther was from the Neanderthal.

To say that Europeans are feudal-insectoid, that Africans are tribal-primates, that Japanese are techno-insectoid, is not to deny the ecological unity

Westward 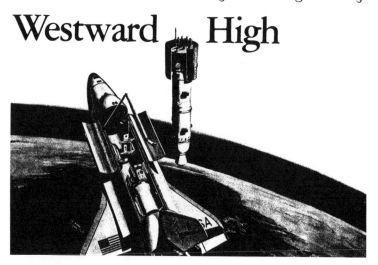 High

of all life on this planet. DNA wants the whales to survive, DNA wants the crafty Middle-Easterners to continue to quarrel over borders. We can respect the ant-hill commitment of the Chinese to the super-insect Mao, and appreciate the technological skill of the web-spinning spidery-electronic Japanese. We can revere our midbrain and spinal links to the Old World and at the same time we must recognize our genetic ascendance beyond our primate, mammalian, insectoid roots.

Arizona and California are states totally populated by migrants squeezed forward by Old World gene-pools. The smart Africans have left Africa and are in America. Futique Mexicans swam the river. The superior Jews landed at Ellis Island along with the genetically selected Germans—all of our ancestors moving to the Sunset Strip in response to the genetic imperative.

Nor are these remarks demeaning to the Old World Old Brain residents. Migration still continues. This week several thousand Blacks, Orientals, Europeans left the Old Brain Hemispheres and carried their ovaries and testicles Westward. If any Old Brain citizen is insulted by these remarks, we repeat the affectionate invitation—if you are genetically selected to advance neurogenetic intelligence on this nursery planet you'll head for the Western Frontier tomorrow.

IF YOU ARE GEARED TO CREATE THE FUTURE GENE-POOLS, MOVE WEST TO JOIN US.

Come on up, you happy Arabs and you mellow Jews
and you clever Africans and you alert Mexicans and
you restless, freedom-loving Orientals. We need
your adventurous intelligence to join us in the next
great migration. Westward High. Regardless of race,
creed, color, national origin—if you are geared to
create the future gene-pools, move West to join us.

We need you up here with us

on the
frontal
lobe of
this
primitive
planet.

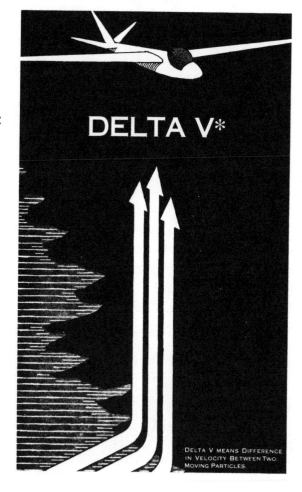

DELTA V*

DELTA V MEANS DIFFERENCE
IN VELOCITY BETWEEN TWO
MOVING PARTICLES.

13

THE HUMAN RACE

TERRESTRIAL POLITICS are rooted Newtonian-Euclidean reality. They are based upon territorial mammalian competitions between neighboring hives who share the same neurotechnological level. Each quantum jump in neurotechnology increases the size of the political unit. Tribes are swallowed up by neighbors who have superior artifacts. Higher technology nations set up territorial boundary tensions of greater extension. In the latter 20th Century China and Russia confronted each other along a 3000-mile border with the same nervous, bluffing robot postures of four-foot mammals protecting turf.

Ideological differences are, of course, irrelevant in mammalian terrestrial politics. The enmity is instinct—robotic. Neighboring gene pools have to compete according to a relentless law of territorial—plus-minus—magnetism.

To occupy an ecological niche is automatically to be "against" those who inhabit the neighboring niche.

To illustrate the limbic, primitive-brain nature of
Old World politics consult the map illustrating the
state of terrestrial politics in the latter 20th Century. We see that Morocco received its arms from
America and that its neighbor, Algeria, obtained
weapons from Russia. The border between the two
neighbors was tense. The next country, Tunisia,
received its arms from America and quarreled with
both its neighbors, leftist Algeria and leftist Libya.
Poor confused Egypt caught between a Black and
White ambiguity switched from Russia to America.
For example, Egypt managed to maintain hostile
contact with both its neighbors—Libya and Israel—
regardless of the ideological paradox!

Africa is a checkerboard of mammalian savagery.

Continuing down the zoo-cages of our animal past,
we note that Israel fought Syria. Syria growled at
Israel above and Iraq below. Iraq fought Iran. Iran
snarled at Afghanistan. Afghanistan frowned at
Pakistan. Pakistan hated India. India tensed against
China. China suspiciously rubbed up against Russia
and the South East Asian states—all of which dis-
trusted their neighbors, regardless of ideology.

   An examination of the politics of Southern Africa
at that time reveals the same checkerboard sequence of neighborhood confrontations. South East
Asia provided a similar confirmation of the theory
that terrestrial politics produces an almost perfect
unbroken sequence of robot mammalian-territorial
confrontations.

A magnetic ordering of plus-minus charges in neighboring units develops. With robot regularity, and with an amazing disregard for common sense or political principles, each country opposes its neighbors. Even the renowned 20th Century political theorist Henry Kissinger failed to understand this neuro-political principle because he was so totally robotized—like iron filings held in a magnetic field—in confrontation with Russia. Kissinger believed in the Domino Theory—if South Vietnam fell, then all the South East Asian nations would topple shoulder-to-shoulder into monolithic Communism.

This paranoia, for which 50,000 young Americans died, completely disregarded the obvious. Once Saigon collapsed then nature took over! Cambodia attacked Vietnam. Vietnam raided Laos. Thailand snarled at Vietnam. And all Southeast Asian countries opposed their northern neighbor China.

NORTH-SOUTH FACTORS

So FAR WE HAVE CONSIDERED the East-West sequence of polarization. Next, let us examine some North-South factors. The map of Africa reveals that the principle of neighbor-antagonism exists. What the political map does not show is the fact that within African countries, which were arbitrarily defined by European colonists, tribal enmities continue to rage on. Africa is a checkerboard of mammalian savagery. Ninety percent of African countries are ruled by assassins and military chiefs. Mafia capos.

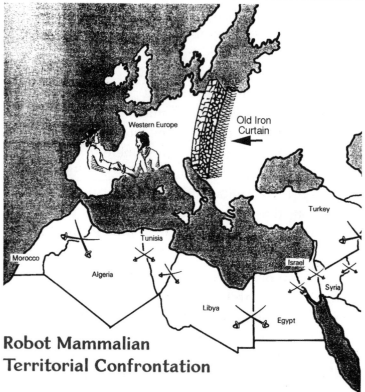

Robot Mammalian
Territorial Confrontation

LOOK NORTH TO EUROPE. Until World War II, Europe was
also a checkerboard of quarreling neighbors, each
ruled by a feudal chief. The technological quantum
leap taken in World War II forced a change in territoriality.

Technology always increases the size of the gene pool territory.

The Eastern Bloc nations were forced together into a
monolithic entity confronting the union of West European states transferring border-tensions from between individual nations to the divide between East
and West—the Iron Curtain. Interestingly, ninety
percent of West European countries are ruled, not by
military dictators, but by elected representatives.

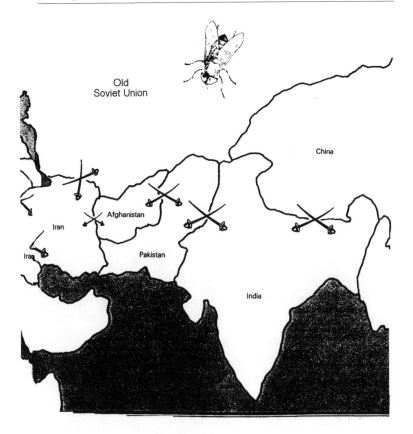

LIKE BRAIN HEMISPHERES

THE NORTH-SOUTH BIFURCATION of the genetic highway
has produced a fascinating left-right division
which perfectly parallels the cerebral hemispheric
split.

Like those who are right-handed, the
northern countries excel at logic,
rationality, and manipulation of artifacts
and symbols.

The new technologies require larger networks of harmonious collaboration. The energies of thousands of people must be linked-up to maintain an automotive business or a Coca-Cola industry. Technology creates larger and more intelligent gene-colony units.

Europe, the right-hand-continent developed the technology and carried the freedom-gene upward. By contrast, the left-hand continent, Africa, failed to produce mobility-freedom-gene pools. Africa developed slavery and Europe developed capitalist-democracy.

The genetic highway veered north instead of south when it burst out of the Middle East—the midbrain.

The northern Mediterranean centers lighted up in sequence—Greece, Rome, Venice, Paris, Madrid, Lisbon, London.

There must be a basic neuro-geographical principle that explains why Africa swarms with slavery and Paleolithic savagery, while the right-hand-northern lobe has provided the centers and pathways along which the species has evolved. We can only speculate as to why the freedom-genes clustered along the North Atlantic beaches and why the intelligence-technology breakout occurred from West Europe and not West Africa.

Think of evolution as an ascent— literally a climb, a series of intelligence tests which activate the velocity-altitude-freedom circuits.

From the Mid-East—
the midbrain—there
are two pathways.
The Southern route
is the easiest. The
Arabs took it and
slid off along the low
road. Insectoid armies oozing from
the East, sending, not gene pools, but soldiers and
military bureaucrats.

By contrast, the highroad North was a ladder, a
series of ledges to be scaled. Look at the map. First
the Dardenelles to be crossed. Then the prickly mountains of Greece, the fingered peninsulas, the Balkan
mountains and the high Alps—rugged land, uninviting
to Mid-Eastern sultans. Choked with geographic
barters offering refuge to ascending gene pools. The
story of evolution is the ascent of Celtic out-caste
gene pools standing on the shoulders of the teeming
Eastern autonomic-involuntary centers.

THE HUMAN RACE

A GLANCE AT THE MAP reminds us that the Human Race is
literally a mobility-contest in which small gene pools
race to keep ahead of the engulfing wave of insectoid
collectivism. The Human Race is exactly a competition
of speed. Small gene pools being squirted ahead by
swarming pressures into empty ecological niches
where new realities—plan-its—can be created. The
Human Race is a run to the West. The Contest is
between the collective and the individual. Can the
individual freedom-gene pools accelerate fast enough
to leave the planet before being overrun by Eastern
hivism?

MOBILITY IS THE KEY
TO INCREASED INTELLIGENCE

The issue is, however, never in doubt. The swarming pressure of the primitive-past lapping at the outskirts of the frontier is simply a signal to speed up. At exactly that moment when the forces of homogenous unity, oneness, socialist-equality, cultural-determinism seem to become dogma—exactly at that moment genetic-elitism reappears among the outpost-outcastes and new gene pools assemble on the frontier outposts. Everyone on the frontier is self-selected for frontier behavior. The new ecological niche is always filled by those who are robot-templated for mobility, independence and change. An important caste to any species.

THE HIGH-ROAD NORTH WAS A LADDER, A SERIES OF LEDGES TO BE SCALED.

Everyone on the frontier is self-selected for frontier behavior—mobility, independence and change.

The ascent of gene pools up the Atlantic in the 16th, 17th, 18th, and 19th Centuries was a genetic-selection process of gigantic significance. It must be recalled that immigration to North America involved an amazing seed blossoming of gene pools. Very few immigrants made the climb alone. Typically, each European gene pool sent its best fertile stock. Once a beachhead had been established in the new ecological niche, more settled members of the gene pools could follow. In most cases, however, new gene pools were formed by mutated-migrants of former Old-World gene pools.

THE HUMAN RACE IS A RUN TO THE WEST.

14

HIGH ORBITAL MIGRATION

*I*N THE 16ᵀᴴ CENTURY the Old World faced the challenging opportunity of colonizing a vast and rich New World. Two psychosocial systems—the Anglo-Celtic and the Mediterranean—set up civilizations in North America and South America respectively.

The Anglo-Celtic psychosocial model is based upon individualism. It emphasizes democratic rule, open communication, free mobility, plurality of lifestyle, personal growth, tolerance of difference, encouragement of invention, competition, experimentation, creativity, decentralization, private enterprise, free-market exchange, and distrust of military authority.

The Mediterranean psychosocial model is derived from Oriental and Middle-Eastern philosophies. It emphasizes subordination of the individual to authoritarian hive-rule; restriction of communication—censorship; restriction of movement, controlled uniformity of lifestyle; discouragement of personal growth; rigid maintenance of herd-tradition; state

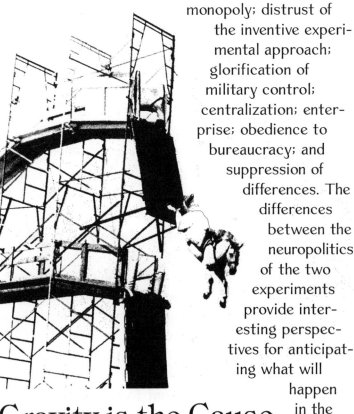

monopoly; distrust of the inventive experimental approach; glorification of military control; centralization; enterprise; obedience to bureaucracy; and suppression of differences. The differences between the neuropolitics of the two experiments provide interesting perspectives for anticipating what will happen in the future as the limitless

Gravity is the Cause of all Suffering.

riches of post-terrestrial space attract Old World social competition.

A brief examination of the evolution of these two social models in South and North America provides instructive suggestions for the future of space colonization. The technological and economic solutions necessary for permanent and highly profitable High Orbital Mini-Earths—H.O.M.E.S.—must be adequately worked out. The future of post-terrestrial Plan-It colonization depends on resolving software

PLAN-IT COLONIES IN HIGH ORBIT PROVIDE A ECOLOGICAL VACUUM IN WHICH HUMAN CASTE DIFFERENCES CAN BLOSSOM.

issues, including mobilization of public opinion supporting free migration, democratic access to available resources. political and cultural control, and psychosocial models and metaphors to guide life in the new custom-made worlds

The best way to avoid the emergence of civil-service bureaucracies, military dictatorships, class struggles, centralized monopolies, impositions of standardized life-styles—the South Amercianization of space—is to reexamine the specific factors that led to the success of the North American model. Emphasis on individuality, the open invitation to migrants from every continent, and free communication made the emergence of a United States possible. It is equally important to review the mistakes made by the North American pioneers.

The prospect of space settlement gracefully harnesses the imagination of freedom loving people throughout the planet.

Many hope to recall, renew, reinvigorate and repeat the successful aspects of the Jeffersonian-Edisonian model. Among these factors are the frontier expansive spirit, the independent, self-actualized western hero-heroine, the small gene pool group seeking to live out a new vision, adventure and calculated risk, the genetic imperative, and the melting-pot open-society mystique. The rugged individual has tremendous allure

SCIENCE FICTION HERO

THE RUGGED INDIVIDUAL HAS TREMENDOUS ALLURE.

IN THE EARLY DECADES OF THE 20TH CENTURY traces of industrial pollution manufactured by domesticated adults initiated the activation of the first post-terrestrial hum-models. Thousands of hedonic networkers were produced in gene pools located in the forward technological niches of Western Europe. Most of these premature evolutes ended up as weirdo artists or in asylums.

The more fortunate appeared in environments where their neural programs could find external supports. Robert Goddard, the Wizard of Worcester, flourished in the Snow Belt of the New World. Konstantin Edouradovich Tsiolovsky, the genius of Kaluga, was produced by a dissenting science intellectual gene pool. Space-visionary Krafft A. Ehricke sprung from parents who were scientifically trained. The most successful of the proto-post-terrestrials was Werner von Braun.

In studying the personal evolution of these mutants, the neurogeneticist is not surprised to discover that during the vulnerable-to-imprint adolescent years, there occurred the revelation, the flash insight that *they were not terrestrials.*

There occurred the revelation, the flash of insight that *they were not terrestrials.*

Goddard's unfolding pre-sexual brain was stimulated, as were millions of preado-lescent lobes, by the science fiction of Jules Verne and by the standard "fantasy" stories of Mars exploration

NEWSPAPERS ARE POWERFUL REALITY-TRANSMISSION TOOLS DURING THE PRE-FLIGHT YEARS.

in daily newspapers. The effect of science fiction and of "yellow journalism" in activating post-terrestrial circuits cannot be overestimated! UFO rumors, Sci-Fi hoaxes, lurid unscientific news stories are key signals which awaken young brains to futique possibilities. Newspapers are powerful reality-transmission tools during the preflight years.

When a newspaper publishes a wild, unfounded hoax story with a science fiction theme, it is performing a key role in evolution by using the hive-ritual of "news" to transmit a future reality trace.

SCIENCE FICTION IS ALWAYS MORE IMPORTANT THAN SCIENCE.

SCIENCE FICTION IS ALWAYS MORE IMPORTANT than science because the former anticipates, guides and directs the latter. Indeed, it is safe to say that all scientific progress is initiated by science fictionists who turn their blueprints over to the science engineers. The Scientist Fiction Caste is the future probe of the species—always pre-dom by many stages. The Hive Engineer Caste is much more numerous.

**SEEK EVOLUTIONARY AGENTS
FROM OTHER GENE POOLS TO
STIMULATE *YOU* TO GET SMARTER.**

For every post-hive science fictionist there are more than a thousand hive science engineers who work on the present and past. Post-hive scientists are rarely called by that name. For example, Jules Verne was called a novelist; Giordano Bruno a dissenting philosopher; Arthur C. Clarke—who designed the Com-Sat system decades before its manufacture—is considered a sci-fi author.

WERNER VON BRAUN

EVOLUTIONARY AGENT WERNER VON BRAUN was born of a noble family in Silesian Germany. Members of pre-dom castes born to aristocratic gene pools at times of technological advance are unusually free to attain stage thirteen Me-generation self-indulgence and stage fourteen self-actualized status and thus choose—i.e., are allowed to follow DNA intuitions—to select their robot-role.

Von Braun's mother, another Evolutionary Agent, encouraged her son to study the stars. *"For my confirmation,"* confided von Braun, *"I got a telescope. My mother thought this would make the best gift."* According to biographer Shirley Thomas, *"Through this hobby, he happened upon an article in an astronomy magazine that crystallized the patterns his life should take. He relates, 'I don't remember the name of the magazine or the author, but the article described an imaginary voyage to the moon. It filled me with a romantic urge. Interplanetary travel! Here was a task worth dedicating one's life to! Not just to stare through a telescope at the moon and the planets but to soar through the heavens and actually explore the mysterious universe. I knew how Columbus had felt.'"*

Reflect on this amazing statement. This preadolescent larval understood how an Evolutionary Agent, who lived 450 years before him, felt about his genetic task. Columbus was clear about his destiny, his obligation to the species. But the significance of his genetic clarity is, of course, lost upon most biographers. That the young von Braun responded to the genetic imperative behind the Columbus mission is comforting evidence that pre-programmed nervous systems can be activated in preadolescence to extraordinary futique missions.

JULES VERNE

THE FATHER OF SCIENCE FICTION, Jules Verne, born February 8, 1828, was recognized, even during his lifetime as an evolutionary fabricator. His novels appeal equally to children and adults, including *Twenty Thousand Leagues Under the Sea* and *Around the World in Eighty Days*, which are still in print more than a century after their publication.

In the years since his death in 1905, Verne emerged as something of a prophet. Among the scientific advances anticipated in his books were the submarine, airplane, television and space travel. Sometimes Verne's prescience could simply be uncanny, as Frank Borman, the American astronaut, discovered after completing the Apollo 8 moon mission. In a letter to Jean Jules-Verne, the author's grandson, Borman wrote: *"It cannot be a mere matter of coincidence. Our space vehicle was launched from Florida, like the spaceship in From the Earth to the Moon; it had the same weight and the same height, and it splashed down in the Pacific a mere two and a half miles from the point mentioned in the novel."*

.

15

GENETIC HISTORY

GENETIC HISTORY, as opposed to political history, is a record of those moments when a successful gene pool migrates in response to swarming pressures when the hive castes out its future probes. The migrating waves produce the highest peaks of civilizations, of culture, of hive philosophy and of art and science.

Civilization began in the East. Shuttling up and down the spinal column from Suez to China. The great pyramids of Egypt remind us that long ago women and men looked at the stars and built enormous highways aloft. Inside the pyramid they assembled all the instruments and comforts needed in a post-terrestrial life. The Egyptian gene pool evolved rapidly and prematurely because they had temporarily solved the four terrestrial survival problems—security, political autonomy, technological predominance and a national sociosexual mythos.

The Nile Valley geography produced this early genetic probe into the future.

CIVILIZATION BEGAN
IN THE EAST

THE EPIC POEM *Gilgamesh* celebrates Babylonian
breakthroughs in science, mathematics, astronomy,
medicine, and technology. Gilgamesh was king of
Uruk who lived about 2700 B.C. on the River
Euphrates in Iraq. He personified the search for the
seed-flower of immortality. His is a story of going
beyond limits, beyond chartered realms, beyond the
territories of the known to scout out gene pool
futures.

Concurrently, when the Greek wave migrated,
Sophocles and Aeschylus wrote their plays; Phidias
sculpted; Socrates, Plato and Aristotle, and the
physical mathematical philosophers raised Greek
civilization to its highest point.

Next, the Intelligence Frontier moved to Rome.
Virgil sang the song of the Migrating Aeneid. All the
great epics are "trip" stories of classic heroes
surfing genetic waves and of voyagers moving out
beyond hive limits. After Rome, the Arab empire
exploded from the Middle East across the North
African coast. The great achievements of the Mos-
lem wave
came in the

universities of Cordoba and Seville where Arab mathematicians, philosophers, musicians and astronomers made their great contributions to the evolution of intelligence. When successful gene pools migrate, expand, explode outward, westward, they propel their seed-style into the future.

For the last 2000 years, a wave of mutation and migration has moved the highest intelligence flower of our species relentlessly from East to West. The Phoenicians, and then the Greeks, pushing their risky spacecraft out across the Mediterranean, their brows cleaving the unknown sea. Marine technology started the movement of gene pools West towards the unknown future.

ALL THE GREAT EPICS ARE "TRIP" STORIES.

The ecological niche inhabited by a gene pool stimulates specific survival skills.

Where you live determines how you behave and how your gene pool evolves. When our marine ancestors crawled out of the water the new ecological niche—the shoreline—activated improved survival tactics involving new, more complex brain circuitry. Different shoreline environments stimulated different neurotechnological skills. Up on land, mobility and communications systems are determined by the climatic and geological considerations of the pathways along which gene pools evolve.

As the importance of geography in shaping human behavior has become clearer, human ethologists have begun to study the effects of migration upon neural development. They have concluded that the location of the large landmasses has an effect in the evolution of human technology. Asians back East manifest survival techniques—especially in social organization and in the amount of power allowed the individual—which are different from Europeans. North Americans are a different species in their behavior from South Americans.

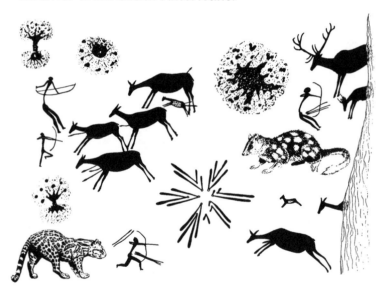

WAS LIFE WAS SEEDED ON THIS PLANET?

WHY ARE WE HERE? How did life get started on this planet? These are crucial questions because your answer determines how you live your life here, and defines your goal. Your answer to the creation question (how you got here) determines what the next stop is, and where you are going.

There are two conventional theories of creation. The first, the scientific, is the most popular now. It is quite mad! It's the Darwinian dogma of accidental, statistical mutation—natural selection. A blind, aimless, accidental forward lurching of evolution.

NATURAL SELECTION IS A BLIND, AIMLESS, ACCIDENTAL FORWARD LURCHING OF EVOLUTION.

Urey and Miller performed an experiment in Chicago years ago. They put ammonium, methane and water vapor in a jar, blasted it with an electrical charge and found prebiotic molecules. Then, they claim that is how life started.

Look at any biological textbook! And marvel at the superstitions of current salaried scientists! Here's the orthodox hive scientific fantasy of evolution: Billions of years ago there was this bunch of methane molecules and they had a parry one night with some ammonia molecules and invited a few carbon girls over, and started drinking water vapor, and the joint got hit by lightning. And they began to copulate! None of the biology textbooks explains self-replication,

by the way. They quickly slide over the key issue. How did prebiotic amino acid become living organism?

Now the other orthodox theory is a vulgar, populist misinterpretation of the *Bible*. I am sure that the pre-civilized writers of the *Bible* didn't mean this, but the parrot-version taught in Sunday School is that life was designed by some kind of police-type Jehovah. An Arab desert macho character who went around interrogating, arresting and condemning anyone that he didn't like, and stationed an Irish cop named Michael at the gate of the Oasis to keep dissidents out.

DIRECTED PANSPERMIA

ANOTHER VIEW IS DIRECTED PANSPERMIA—the theory that life was seeded on this planet by higher intelligence and evolves, stage by stage, according to a preprogrammed plan. The Panspermia theory was developed by a Swedish biologist named Svante Arrhenius who suggested that this planet was seeded by spores from outer space. Dozens of pre-biotic-organic molecules have been found floating around in pre-stellar cloud complexes and in a type of meteorite called carbonacious chrondites.

The French were uninterested in Panspermia until they discovered that alcohol was one of the biological molecules in space. Paris Match immediately ran an article on the existence of extra-terrestrial intelligence!

Then in 1973, a distinguished scientist, a geneticist named Sir Francis Crick—he decoded the DNA code with Watson—and his colleague Orgel suggested the theory of *Directed Panspermia:* This planet may have been deliberately seeded. It is possible, and it is certainly fun to believe, that there are millions or even billions of planets like ours in this small galaxy alone, that have been similarly seeded. And that the same process of evolution is taking place here and on many other planets.

This planet may have been deliberately seeded.

Some sophisticated geneticists now agree with the Panspermia theory because they say it is impossible that in two and a half billion years, accidental copying-error mutations could have taken us from simple, unicellular life to Monday night football and Howard Cosell.

DNA DOES NOT PLAY DICE WITH THE UNIVERSE

AND

WHO SEEDED US HERE

ON THIS WOMB

PLANET?

WE,

IN THE FUTURE,

DID IT!

16

NEUROGEOGRAPHICAL DETERMINISM

ACCORDING TO WEGNER'S THEORIES of continental drift in the beginning there was one landmass on the planet—Gonawanda. This one blob of extruded rock split into continents. Inertia from planet-spin, West to East, pulled the continents a part. The continents and hemispheres of planet Earth have been settled by technological civilizations in stages which correspond to the evolution of brain centers. Thus the arrangement of landmasses corresponds topologically to the anatomy of the nervous system. Asia is the spinal column; the Middle East is the mid-brain, and the limbic system; Europe and Africa are containers for the right and left lobes of the old cortex; North and South America are platforms for the emergence of the neocortex, the self-defining future brain.

When we chart the emergence of civilization, the emergence of increasingly complex technology and social-communication systems, it is apparent that different continents were activated at different times in history—Asia, then Europe, then America.

The migration of human populations from Eastern to Western continents corresponds to the emergence of more evolved brain centers. Landmasses are literally platforms for emerging brain circuits. The distribution of landmass is an external representation of evolving brain circuits.

THE MIGRATION OF NEUROTECHNOLOGY FROM CONTINENT TO CONTINENT HAS CLOSELY PARALLELED THE OPENING-UP OF NEW NEURAL PATHWAYS.

Establishment of population centers in Western areas paralleled the emergency of high-more-frontal brain centers. The new migratory pathways, probing Westward, correspond to the direction of neural pathways up from the spinal column, to the mid-brain, to the limbic system, to the cortex, to the frontal cortex. The landmasses of the planet earth serve as container-niches for newly emerging brain circuits. Geography from the evolutionary point of view, is literally topological neuroanatomy.

From the evolutionary point of view, geography is topological neuroanatomy.

The problem in understanding neurogeography is that neurologicians do not have a clear picture of the centers and pathways of the human nervous system. As they become more precise in locating brain functions then the correspondence with ecological-niche-containers will be more precisely described. All we can do is to simply sketch in the striking similarities between geography and brain circuit.

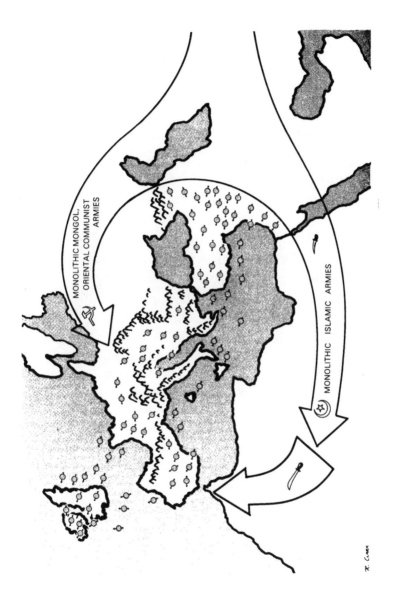

SPINAL CORD

THE AUTONOMIC NERVOUS SYSTEM runs from
China to the Middle-East. The autonomic
nervous system regulates involuntary
action. This ancient brain includes the
spinal cord, the medulla and pons which
comprise the hindbrain and the midbrain.

   Historically we know that human civilization emerged in the Middle East around
4200 BC and for four thousand years was
centered in cities stretching from China
to the Middle East, flowing along trade-
route-invasion pathways. This region of
the globe—like the spinal column—has
always stressed involuntary behavior,
discouraging and limiting individual-
voluntary behavior.

MIDBRAIN

THE REPTILIAN-MAMMALIAN NERVOUS SYSTEM—midbrain—is
located in the middle east. The so-called reptile
brain—R complex—is made up of circuits which sur-
round the midbrain and according to Carl Sagan "plays
an important role in aggressive behavior, territoriality,
ritual and the establishment of social hierarchies." Also
surrounding the midbrain is the limbic area which
"appears to generate strong or particularly vivid
emotions. . . and the beginnings of altruistic behavior."

   The area just west of—above—Asia emerged as the
dominant-civilization around 300 B.C. This Mid-East
region continues to be a center of territorial disputes,
jealousies, revenges and passionate conflict among
neighbors and social hierarchies.

LEFT AND RIGHT CORTEX

THE POSTERIOR CORTEX is located in Africa-Europe. At this point in our charting of neurogeography we consider two major fissurings of the global landmass. The Mediterranean Sea separates Africa from Europe. The Mediterranean corresponds to the longitudinal cerebral fissures—known as the median sagittal groove—which divides the cortex into the left and right brains. The left cortex mediates the right side of the body. Thus the left cortex is Europe and the right cortex is Africa. The two neurogeographical hemispheres are linked at Gibraltar.

The second fissuring of the global landmass is the separation of the forward parts of Africa and Europe, which—floating across the enormous sulcus called the Atlantic Ocean—created two large lobes of land, neuro-technically quiescent but ready for future innervation. Innervation means to supply a bodily part with nerves.

The European right-hand mediates rational, logical, mathematical, linear, disciplined behavior. The African left-hand mediates intuitive, nonlinear, patterned-rhythmic behavior. The left cortex is involved in manufacture of artifacts. The right cortex is involved in neurosomatic behavior. The left cortex is scientific. The right cortex magic. To understand more precisely the evolutionary stage of the European reality it is useful to contrast it with the next stage—the prefrontal American mutation.

THE LEFT CORTEX IS EUROPE; THE RIGHT CORTEX IS AFRICA.

FRONTAL LOBES

THE FRONTAL LOBES OF THE CORTEX are the most recent
additions to the brain's neuroanatomical structure.
Embryologically, the old cortex develops and splits
into hemispheres by the fourth month of pregnancy.
But the overarching, forward pushing frontal lobes
only emerge just before birth—which is where we
are now—just before birth!

North and South America are containers for the neocortex—the emerging frontal lobes of the brain.

For decades the prevailing view of neurophysiolo-
gists was that the frontal lobes, which are behind
the forehead, are the sites of anticipation and plan-
ning for the future. However, the situation is not so
simple. A large number of cases of frontal lesions
were investigated by Hans-Lukas Teuber of the
Massachusetts Institute of Technology who found
that many frontal lobe lesions have almost no obvious effects on behavior. However, in severe pathology of the frontal lobes "the patient is not alto-
gether devoid of the capacity to anticipate a course
of events, but cannot picture himself in relation to
those events as a potential agent."

This corresponds to two neurogeographic observations. The newest lobe of the cortex appar-
ently involves seeing oneself as a potential agent.

THE MOST RECENT ECOLOGICAL NICHE FOR THE HUMAN SPECIES—THE SO-CALLED NEW WORLD—WAS ACTIVATED AFTER 1492.

To West America—the left-lobe right-hand of the
neuro-map—came floods of self-selected gene pools.
A basic characteristic of the American-conscious-
ness is "future-orientation." North America was
settled by gene pools self-selected for future reality
fabrication and self-reliant independence. Old World
visitors are always amazed at the American trust in
progress and the optimism of individual-identity.

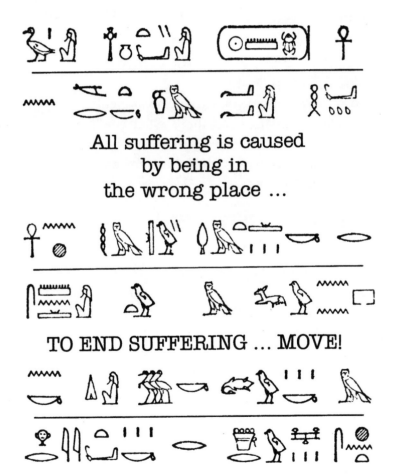

All suffering is caused
by being in
the wrong place ...

TO END SUFFERING ... MOVE!

Determinism

NEUROGEOGRAPHICAL LOCATION DETERMINES the stage of
neuroevolution. If you could voyage around the brain
you would find that where you are determines what
you are doing and thinking. If you are in the midbrain you expect everyone to be running around
concerned with mid-brain functions—territoriality.
We expect the Mid-East
to be involved in mid-   **WHERE YOU ARE**
brain functions—and they **DETERMINES WHAT**
are Arab-Zionist mam-   **YOU ARE DOING**
malian competition.   **AND THINKING.**

When you trip South
to the African cortex you expect nonlogical, intuitive, magical thinking—and that's what you'll find.
When you climb up to the left-frontal lobe you
expect to find concern with the future—and that's
what we find in America.

THE BAWDY PILGRIMS

THE PASSENGERS ON THE MAYFLOWER were not stern,
straightlaced, middle-aged religious zealots. The
stuffy ones were Puritans, and they remained in
Britain, protesting what they considered to be the
liberal ways of the Church of England.

The Pilgrims were mostly young Elizabethans in
their twenties and thirties. They wore colorful
clothes, not those black hats and gray gowns you
see in the paintings. They enjoyed good times,
including the imbibing of strong spirits and the
telling of bawdy stories.

Not only did they believe in a simple form of worship without trappings and fanfare; they also believed strongly in individual freedom and—here's an important part of their success story—they became devoted capitalists two years after their arrival at Plymouth Rock.

On the ninth day they rounded the tip of Provincetown and the Mayflower dropped anchor in Cape Cod Bay; the Pilgrims sat down together and drafted the first written covenant calling for civil self-government and individual freedom. Independence was born. It was the forerunner of the United States Constitution. It was the Mayflower Compact.

Because the Pilgrims hadn't possessed enough money to rent and provision the Mayflower for its lengthy voyage, they financed their trip with the help of profit-seeking British businessmen. The Pilgrims agreed to work for the profit of a joint stock company. They were to invest their labor, and share in the profits. The London merchants were to invest their money and also share in the profits.

It was the night independence was born.

Each Pilgrim received a share of stock. Everything that was produced was to go into a common fund. At the end of seven years they were to sell whatever was left, beyond the necessities of living, and divide the proceeds according to the distribution of the shares of stock.

The British investors had demanded a communal setup in the New World. It would make the distribution of profits and land much more convenient at the end of the seven years of the contract.

17

INDIVIDUAL FREEDOM

IN THE 19TH CENTURY the British Empire performed extraordinary feats of genetic transportation—squirting sperm-egg cargoes throughout the globe. By moving their dom-species domesticated adult Protestants from Scotland to Ireland, they ruthlessly compressed the barbarian teenager Catholic-feudal culture of the Emerald Isle. Faced with loss of the land Catholic gene pools were forced to migrate. Each Irish family selected its most intelligent, mobile, adaptable, attractive member to send "across the water". Thus occurred one of the most successful genetic experiments in planetary history.

AMERICA WAS FLOODED WITH SPERM-EGG UNITS CAREFULLY SELECTED FOR MOBILITY-NOBILITY.

The first generation of Irish migrants threw railroads across the continent. The second generation became politicians, policers, power functionaries. The third generation, which blossomed after World War II, produced the first Irish-American generation of philosopher-scientists.

The brilliant, innovative Irish servants who emerged in the mid-20th Century replaced the Jewish intellectuals. Before that Jewish intellectuals carried the neurogenetic signal.

Since Jews were born Out-Castes they were able to transcend hive limits and fabricate new realities.

After World War II Jewish culture became hive establishment and the role of genetic exploration fell to the Irish. The American Celts were prepared perfectly to play the role of Evolutionary Agents because of their intellectual history. In premigration Ireland the active intellectual person was forced into rebellion. The only educational choices for smart, young Irishmen were the alien, Rome-oriented feudal priesthood or the academies of the enemy Protestants. Young Irish women had no educational avenues open to them. Irish brains were thus encouraged to be anti-hive. From this out-caste position they were able to create new post-hive realities.

Different sites for different rites

KEEP JUST AHEAD OF THE WAVE

THE QUESTION OF WHERE IS EASILY ANSWERED. Find the genetic runway on your planet, face the setting sun and move West. To find the genetic river, first locate your heart. Since it is on your left side, you know you will manipulate with your right hand. The large land mass is to your right when you face the setting sun.

Face West at the shadow. Move between the swamp on your left and the iceberg on your right. On other planets spin-eccentricity slides the big

DON'T GET BOGGED DOWN IN THE HOT SWAMPS TO YOUR LEFT.

land-mass south. Then all left-right north-south codes are reversed. This is a galactic constant. The Heart is always located on the equator-side when you move West. For Protection. The superior-technology-danger always comes from the north. The right hand hunts. The left hand is used for gathering. You will find the fruit trees growing on your south side.

The question of how is already settled. Keep just ahead of the wave. Use the West-Ward ecological niche as base. Don't get bogged down in the hot swamps to your left. Don't get frozen in the structures to your right.

So the only question is when? Since everything spirals through the 24 Stage cycle, simply locate your spot on the species-cycle, the cultural history cycle, and the personal-individual cycle and keep moving up-ward and outward at increasing velocity, making more precise linkups."

INDIVIDUAL FREEDOM IS THE KEY TO EVOLUTION

History, indeed, evolution itself, can be charted in terms of the growth of freedom-of-the-individual.

FREEDOM

1. Amount of mobility—velocity-altitude, and communicaiton-scope attained by the individual.

2. Amount of direciton-control of transportation-communication attained by the individual.

3. The opportunity of free-responsible individuals to signal each other and link-up in ore complex networks inevitably leading to migraiton.

KEY TO EVOLUTION

HISTORY, INDEED, EVOLUTION ITSELF, can be charted in terms of the growth of freedom-of-the-individual. It is the amount of direction-control of transportation-communication attained by the individual. It is the opportunity of free-responsible individuals to signal each other and link-up in more complex networks inevitably leading to migration.

FREEDOM IS DEFINED AS THE AMOUNT OF MOBILITY—VELOCITY-ALTITUDE, AND COMMUNICATION-SCOPE ATTAINED BY THE INDIVIDUAL.

It is fashionable for intellectuals to complain about humanity's destructive and pessimistic trend. While, in all charity we can understand the hive meaning of this pessimism, it is the task of Evolutionary Agents to counter it by repeatedly showing that the genetic plan is working out perfectly. The human cards are in no position to interfere with the DNA deal. Remember that for the last 5000 years—a mere micro-flick in genetic time—the species havs been in a continual frenzy of mutation and migration.

A species, or an individual without genetic consciousness, caught in the midst of all-out-high-velocity changes, buffeted, overwhelmed by no-let-up metamorphosis, pushed into rapid migration, is understandably confused and a bit fatigued.

Does a butterfly understand what's happening when it bursts, twisting and dewey-damp out of the dark, cozy cocoon?

There are no maps to describe how it feels during the high-point of mutation. Does a salmon understand what's happening when it is being squeezed back up the Columbia River, battered, pushed against the current, leaping rocks, flipping forward, upward? Does a butterfly understand what's happening when it bursts, twisting and dewy-damp out of the dark, cozy cocoon?

Such dramatic migrations and metamorphoses are simple transitions compared to the bewildering, bumpy voyage of the individual humans and human gene pools in the last several generations.

The human brain goes through extraordinary changes. After nine months of exciting embryonic metamorphosis, it is squeezed into terrestrial life as a peculiar, slug-like larval with an enormous head and shrunken, totally helpless body. The amoeboid-bliss of the neonate is shortly

THE HUMAN BEING IS IN CONTINUAL METAMORPHOSIS.

shattered by the activation of new neural circuits and the sequence of dramatic changes in physiology—biting, crawling, walking, running, talking. Compared to every other species, the human being is in continual metamorphosis. Indeed, the outstanding neurogenetic characteristic of the human is this continual larval change—Homo protean.

In addition to this developmental variability, those who have lived through the 20th Century have been whirled through a sequence of historical changes unparalleled on this womb-planet. A person born in 1900 moved from horse-carriages to Soyuz-

Apollo in one lifetime. From gaslight to nuclear
fusion. Mutations-migrations occur in cycles. Each
generation since 1900 has ridden a series of enormous waves—all-changing reality breakers, with no
chance to catch a breath. Thus, for the first time in
human history, we have some dozen mutant groups
swirling around at the same time—and aware of
each other's changes via electromagnetic communication. Those who just barely, gasping, made it
from the Spanish-American War through World War
I were then asked, with no respite, to deal with the
Roaring Twenties, Communism, the Depression,
Hitler, World War II, Hiroshima, Cold War, television, Lunar landings, drugs, *Hustler*, cloning. No one
has been permitted to stand still.

It's a dizzying, Einsteinian exercise in relativity—
totally bewildering to a species that had been
assured by Newton that every action had an equal
and opposite reaction. Nope, no more.

DISCLOSURE

I have to apologize to you. Please, do not believe
anything I say.

The human nervous system, this 111-billion-cell
bioelectric computer, is not a set of ice tongs.
You don't hook the sharp claws of belief onto an
idea and hold it.

By all means listen to everything; consider anything. Pick up a belief and try it out. If it works,
use it as long as it works. And then put it down or
change it. Be open to new ideas. But I urge you,
don't believe in any final sense anything I say.

The new rule is that every action leads to a multiple interaction, intersection. It's all waves to surf, moving faster and higher.

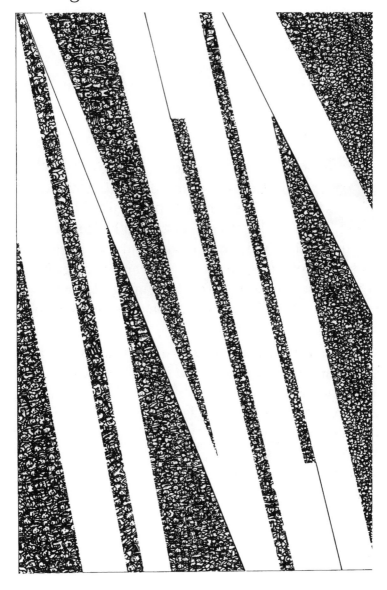

18

HUMAN GENE POOL EX-PLOSION

EVOLUTION IS SPEEDING UP. 20th Century evolution accelerated with a rapidity that is almost impossible for us to understand. The chart stands out as the symbol of our mutational century. It presents the course of evolution in terms of the growth of intelligence—energies received, integrated and transmitted by different geographical subspecies of Homo sapiens.

The chart illustrates that for three billion years the intelligence of life forms on this planet grew with almost invisible acceleration. It took more than two billion years to slowly evolve the muscular technologies that propelled animals a few miles per hour and which produced the muscular force of an elephant.

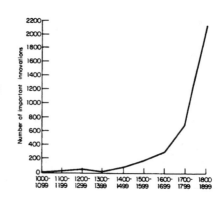

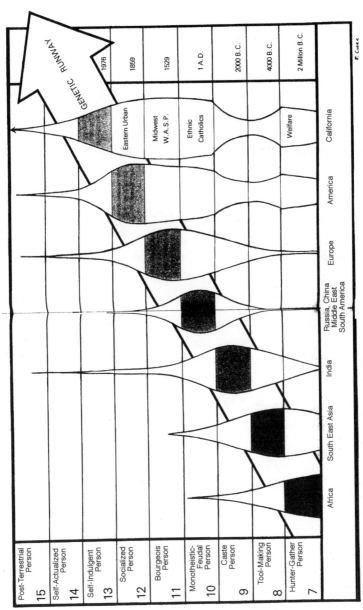

THE GENETIC RUNWAY

Then, with the mechanical revolution, the curve
rockets upward. The horizontal axis of is time indexed
in billions of years. The vertical/energy axis can be
calibrated in terms of number of inventions, energy
produced and con-
THE HUMAN SPECIES IS sumed, mobility in
RIDING AN ENERGY- terms of speed and
INTELLIGENCE BOOM altitude, expansions
of perception—
microscopic or telescopic. Whatever energy index we
chart, the climb rate shot up almost vertically after
1946.

The human species is riding an energy-intelligence
boom that has dramatically changed our conceptions
of evolution. Darwinian theories of blind natural selection are now seen as primitive chauvinism of 19th
Century British imperialism.

Next consider The Genetic Highway. Here the
horizontal axis scopes the neurographic time zones—
from primitive, prehistoric Africa to current California.
The vertical axis is calibrated in DNA time.

The dom-species in Africa is hunter-gatherer. The
Africans are thus two million years behind California—
the Western Front. In Western Europe the dom-species is domesticated adult bourgeois—roughly 400
years behind those on the Western Front.

It is interesting to observe that Africa lacks the
more civilized gene-colonies and that Europe and
Russia and China lack the mammalian-primitive gene-
colonies.

Europe is left brain.
Africa is right brain.

The forcible injection of the powerful African gene strain into North America, via slavery, produced the sturdy, solid, far ranging American and Californian cultures. Post-terrestrial colonization, obviously, must propel seeds from all terrestrial gene pools into High Orbital Mini-Earths—HOMES. The importance of the Black-and-Brown infiltrations into North America and, particularly into California, cannot be overestimated.

HENRY FORD

THE GENETIC WAVE, that in less than a century hurtled North Americans through three stages of evolution, was gleefully surfed by several Evolutionary Agents. One of the most successful was Henry Ford.

In one generation, Agent Ford took a species of domesticated primates from behind horse drawn plows and popped them into mechanical ground-vehicles constructed of steel, glass and rubber—thus multiplying their intelligence.

Ford put his countrymen and countrywomen into the driver's seat! He offered the driver's seat—Throne of Self-Actualization—to the average working hum-ants of his gene pool. It came equipped with several self-actualizing technologies permitting neurological choice and stimulating Intelligence Increase.

The steering wheel allowed individuals to select their own directional course, and to change it at will. The accelerator allowed individuals to select their speed—an Einsteinian concept, indeed. Brakes added another dimension to self-control. Gear shifts. Transmission. Self-starters. Fluid power. Dynaflow. Overdrive. Convertibles.

We see the birth of a new language of self-determination. Succeeding generations demanded for their bodies and their brains exactly those power-freedom-mobility characteristics that were built into our cars.

As the greatest stroke of genetic public relations, Ford called his invention the automobile! This word means self-mover. Evolutionary Agents all over the galaxy **AUTO** smiled knowingly when the term *automobile* **MOBILE** flashed out through the Van Allen Belt.

Free-wheeling Americans called it the self-mover! Old World Europeans, of course, didn't catch on. To them the auto-mobile was another luxury for the rich. It was called horseless carriage in England. Coche in Spain. Carro in Mexico. Voiture in France. Màccina in Italy. The genetic implications of auto-mobile were endless. Average people could move their bodies or their brains where they wanted to go.

The evolution of intelligence is a function of velocity and mobility. Henry Ford and his fellow agents rocketed the Genetic Intelligence Quotient of the species.

When the technological primates climbed into the driver's seat they were soon off to the moon —
carrying their automobile bodies and their automobile brains.

19

HOW FRIENDS BECOME ALIENS

NEIL FREER IS FAMOUS in galactic neurogenetic textbooks because he was the first Earth-Born to activate, master and link-up all twenty four stages of his brain. The extraordinary aesthetic intensity of his temporal caste-stages—which kept his developmental momentum going—won the admiration of dramatists for several centuries.

As a barbarian teenager, Freer's adolescent searching led him to become a Trappist Monk and to make a commitment to his ancient feudal sex-role. As a domesticated adult, evolving from monotheism, Freer became a dedicated husband and father of six children. As a retiring elder, Freer saw the implications of neurotransmitter drugs and was thus able to avoid terminal adulthood and social security hive identification.

Subsequent re-imprinting experiences allowed Freer as a Me-generation grown-up, as a self-actualized adult and as a hedonic networker to sequentially return to post-hive infancy—self-indulgence,

**ALL THE REALITIES WE SHALL EVER KNOW ARE
CREATED BY THE CONVERSATION BETWEEN DNA
AND CNS (CENTRAL NERVOUS SYSTEM).
THE DNA BLUEPRINT OF EVOLUTION,
PAST AND FUTURE, CAN BE DECIPHERED
AS WE TAP INTO THE DNA-CNS CHANNEL.**

self-actualization and a new post-hive link-up with his mate, Ursula. Freer pointed out the signs of an emerging racial post-domestic imprint around age thirty-five.

Freer's systematic activation of neural circuits at the brain reality consumer, the brain reality self-actualized and the brain reality fused stages and his disciplined study of Einsteinian and post-Einsteinian texts allowed him to become the most advanced physicist of the 21st Century. His technique was simple. He opened the neuroelectric circuits with LSD, experienced the patterns and then applied the current mathematical models to create new realities.

Freer performed the same cycle of opening-integration fusion at the neurogenetic circuit. He used LSD to open up the DNA-CNS conversation and then used the current micro-genetic findings to externally describe his experience. Freer developed the concept of dyadic evolution—male/female fusion—moving up the evolutionary scale together.

By the year 2033, Freer became the first Earth-born entity to experience quantum-field contelligence by achieving the stages of quantum consumer, quantum intelligence and twenty four neuro-atomic fusion. His disappearance, with his wife Ursula, into the Black Hole of his own device followed shortly thereafter.

DIFFERENT EVOLUTION

TERRESTRIAL IN ME-GENERATION ECO-NICHES are about ready to deal with the following relativistic facts of their genetic history. They can realize that at earlier, larval stages of their own metamorphosis they shared neuro-realities with those who later grow up to be in very different castes. They can logically accept that, as they develop, their close childhood companions evolve into alien intelligences. We grew and changed, leaving the unicellular neighbors behind.

At one time, shortly after conception, we were all unicellular organisms drifting passively down uterine canals along with trillions of other amoeboid floaters.

TERRESTRIALS! Each time you develop to a new stage you migrate to a new ecological niche. You join a new gene pool. Each time you activate a new stage you say farewell to the neighbors with whom you shared the old hive-reality. "Good-bye, Old Friends, it's time to grow."

Can you remember your best friend in first grade when your temporal caste was monkey? Where is that childhood friend now? Early caste associates become total strangers in years to come.

Consider two six-year old buddies. One is more muscular, more aggressive and confident, more mature in dealing with six-year-old Paleolith reality. First graders know exactly where they fit into the pecking order. But by age sixteen the stronger one can no longer evolve so he quits school to be a truck driver, while the other one goes on to M.I.T. and continues to change and grow, eventually winning the Nobel Prize in Physics. At age 50 the two live in very different realities, competitive gene pools and their brain circuitry is several mutations different.

The skilled laborer operates with a Paleolithic brain capable of skillful mimicry but not inventive thinking. At age six the Nobel Prizer was envious of and intimidated by the muscular superiority of the friend. Age six is the Paleolithic stage in the evolving human brain. The future laborer is templated for superstitious, mimicking-repetitious survival tech-

MESSIAHS, GURUS AND SIMILAR GENE-POOL NAVIGATORS ARE JUDGED BY THE ACCURACY OF THE EVOLUTIONARY MAPS THEY TRANSMIT.

niques, can imitate group rituals, repeat the magic taboo words of the hive, perform complex-rote tasks, handle technology, and twist the dials of his TV set. He can go to the ballot box and dutifully pull a voting lever. But at the core he is a hunter-gatherer surviving confusedly in a technological society.

REALITY JUMPS

THE HIGHER THE HUMAN NEUROGENETIC CASTE, the more mobile the individual. Neural Caste is determined by voluntary mobility. The freer you are to "come and go," the higher your intelligence. Metamorphosis to a higher stage involves movement to a new ecological niche.

The higher the human neurogenetic caste, the more mobile the individual.

This process of movement involves wrenching "good-byes" to those who shared the former niche—and the earlier stage of development. It is necessary that you make linkages at each stage of reality. Indeed, you must master each neural circuit before you can advance.

The twenty four neurogenetic stages are motels up the highway of evolution—centers and pathways up through the global brain. At certain fuel-rest stops we form crew-linkages to lift us up to the next stage. The flight plan of evolution is a series of reality jumps where we cooperate with those in our present reality to help us ascend to the next.

THE FREER YOU ARE TO "COME AND GO," THE HIGHER YOUR INTELLIGENCE.

MATRIMONIAL FUSION

THE DOMESTICATED ADULT MARRIAGE is such a reality jump. It should be clear now that very different mating procedures operate at different stages of neuro-development, The retiring elder marriage is state controlled. Barbarian teenager marriage is a feudal arrangement. Group-minded preadolescent marriage is priest-caste managed. Parrot-brained mimic marriage is bull-harem.

Imagine two lusty, romantic barbarians from the domesticated adult gene pools meet at the High School Prom and decide to make the big jump up to parental reality. They form a two-person flight crew.

MARRIAGE IS A TWO-PERSON FLIGHT CREW.

The marriage ceremony is a metamorphic-migration Cape Canaveral ritual. The bride and groom blast up together—in a flare of rice with tin cans tied to the migration rocket—headed for a new plan-it called Matrimonial Fusion.

After passing the Moon of Honey they eventually arrive, sometimes joltingly, in the New World where they discover that the metamorphosis has produced unexpected forms. As horny teenagers they shared the same sperm-egg reality. As responsible parents they discover that they are a very different species. The shy youth has become an aggressive, selfish father-type barking orders to his astonished mate. And the flamboyant, carefree, go-go teenage girl has become a serious, mature worrier.

Marriage is a Sci-Fi thriller

Two larvals walk hand-in-hand into the Time Transformer not knowing what sort of postlarval forms will emerge. And the contract cunningly says, "until death do you part." After softlanding on the Honey Moon the two aliens wake up in the same bed—strangers from different species. But they must stick together to survive in the domesticated ant-hill.

SEQUENCE OF EVOLUTIONARY FUSION

To METAMORPHOSE from one circuit to another requires fusion. Each circuit of the brain fabricates new realities and a new ecological niche for gene pools formed by mutants from the past hives.

Circuit I—MARINE MUSCULAR TECHNOLOGY: .
[Stages 1 Amoeboid, 2 Fish-Brained, and 3 Lizard-Brained] Eventually the masters of Circuit —the stage three Amphibians—leave the fish marine reality and migrate to form new land-based gene pools.

CIRCUIT II—TERRESTRIAL MUSCULAR TECHNOLOGY.
[Stages 4 Rodent-Brained, 5 Mammalian-
Brained, and 6 Monkey-Brained] Eventually
the Circuit II successes—the stage six gestur-
ing-arboreal primates—leave the four-footed
mammals and move to form new gene pools
based on....

CIRCUIT III—ARTIFACT TECHNOLOGY.
[Stages 7 Parrot-Brained, 8 Thinking Juvenile-
Brained, and 9 Group-Minded Pre-Adolescent-
Brained] Eventually the technological successes—the stage nine caste-linked artisans
and commercial dealers—leave tribal reality
and migrate to form new, collective gene
pools.

CIRCUIT IV—CULTURAL TECHNOLOGY.
[Stages 10 Barbarian Teenager-Brained, 11
Domesticated Adult-Brained, and 12 Retiring
Elder-Brained] Then the Circuit IV urban
masters, the Sun Belt Americans, leave Demo-
poll Welfare-Socialist Society and move to...

CIRCUIT V—SELF-ACTUALIZED BODY TECHNOLOGY.
[Stages 13 Me-Generation-Brained, 14 Self-
Actualized-Brained, and 15 Hedonic
Networker-Brained] Then Circuit V successes
figure out that H.O.M.E.'s are the only escape
from the Encroaching Primitive terrestrial
past and they move to...

CIRCUIT VI—SELF-ACTUALIZED BRAIN TECHNOLOGY.
[Stages 16 Brain-Reality Consumer, 17 Brain
Reality Self-Actualized and 18 Brain Reality
Fused] Eventually the Circuit VI successes
realize that genetic control—involving rejuve-

nation cloning and DNA engineering—is the
next evolutionary step and move to...

CIRCUIT VII—NEURO-GENETIC TECHNOLOGY.
[Stages 19 Genetic Consumer, 20 Genetic
Engineer, and 21 Genetic Symbiosis] Eventually the Stage 21 Genetic-Masters realize that
it is necessary to attain post-psychological
status and move to...

CIRCUIT VIII—QUANTUM-FIELD TECHNOLOGY.
[(Stages 22 Quantum Consumer, 23 Quan-
tum Intelligence and 24 Neuro-Atomic
Fusion]

GENE POOLS MIGRATE across the desert of space-time to
the next oasis. When you have metamorphosed to a
new niche using new technologies your selection and
mastery of the new technologies are an individual
caste choice. Gene pool movement to a new niche is
communal, however. The Scout
Caste can move way out into the   **MIGRATION-**
future and come back to demon-   **MUTATION**
strate the safety of the future-   **CANNOT BE**
pathways, to show that it can be   **PERFORMED**
done. But the work of fabricating   **ALONE**
the new reality involves linkage into
gene pools.

   The voyage of evolution, of a species or of individuals, is a series of linkages and separations. At each
stage of development we synergistically use each
other to grow and move on. We link with our teenage
steady to explore sexual impersonation roles. And then
we move on—and on! And on!

The planet is evolving harmoniously. The dom-species Me-generation grown-up is at present relaxed and reasonably secure. The presence of an enormous growing population of pre-dom future-oriented humans make it

THIS IS A MOST FAST-MOVING, VOLATILE TIME IN THE EVOLUTION OF LIFE ON EARTH.

possible to look realistically at the futures that can be fabricated by this explosive gene colony. This is a most fast-moving, volatile time in the evolution of Life on Earth. Every attempt must be made to give terrestrials future-maps that will allow them to anticipate what is to come—with enthusiasm and intelligence.

20

INFILTRATE THE
FUTURE!

OCATE THE NEUROGENETIC CENTERS where the future
action is happening. There you will find Evolutionary Agents—the Out-Castes. Counter-
Evolutionary Agents consistently make the
mistake of focusing on today's bureaucrat-power-
holders, who are already outdated by the predom
species. In slow moving pre-
technological eras this was
a passable strategy.
Evolutionary Agents
always focus on the
predom species—the
stages to come.
Aristotle hung out
with the teenage
Alexander of
Macedon, not
the reigning
Philip.

EVOLUTIONARY AGENTS ALWAYS FOCUS ON THE PREDOM SPECIES—THE STAGES TO COME.

Locate the Western Frontier centers and exchange signals with the youthful elite who are always visible in frontal-lobe regions. In every terrestrial society there are pupal training centers to which the most successful gene pools send their most intelligent larvals. The future of each gene pool is blueprinted in the minds of its superior adolescents. Teenage brains are the hatcheries of future-realities.

Teenage brains are the hatcheries of future-realities

In Eastern countries you will find university students docile and insectoid obedient. Guess what this hive devotion predicts for the future of China. In the midbrain Sematic countries you will find university students violently nationalistic and fanatically patriotic. In French elite academies you will find serious technocrats. Mon Dieu imagine what that means for the future of France. Tant Pis. At the frontal lobe Sun Belt Universities you will find the young of the predom species obsessed with disciplined self-actualized hedonic freedom.

Sign up for the college lecture circuit on the Western Front. There you will learn what is going to happen. And perhaps, maybe, you can influence this hatching future a tiny, tiny bit.

THE YOUNG OF THE PREDOM SPECIES ARE OBSESSED WITH DISCIPLINED SELF-ACTUALIZED HEDONIC FREEDOM.

WHERE TO FROM HERE?

LIBERATION OF THE BODY is now a dom-species conven-
tion. A sizable predom elite is learning how to use
their brains. This is neurogenetic progress. Self-
actualization of body and brain are basic tools for
creating future plan-its. Post-terrestrial futures can
only be fabricated by women and men who have
pride in their bodies, who understand how to use
and direct their bodies precisely, and who can fuse
their aesthetics in exquisite love linkages with
others.

   To move confidently into the future we must be
guided by women and men who understand that we
can control and change our own realities by the
responsible, self-actualized use of our brains.

When the Mutation Time comes, those who
don't want to be mutated can leave.

LIFT UP YOUR EYES!

Has the DNA code labored (or played) for two and a half billion years to produce as final product, you, the second post-Hiroshima generation, suntanned, languorous, post-political, sophisticated, laid back, affluent, polymorphous orgasm, self-actualized, sensory consumers?

You have arrived at this state of intelligent self-control and responsible self-expression, but I know that you want your evolution to continue. In the second stage of this program we shall learn how to S.M.I. L.E. We shall consider three ideas that, ready or not, like it or not, will determine the future of every gene-pool on the planet.

DNA CODE LABORED (OR PLAYED) FOR TWO AND A HALF BILLION YEARS TO PRODUCE ITS FINAL PRODUCT:

YOU

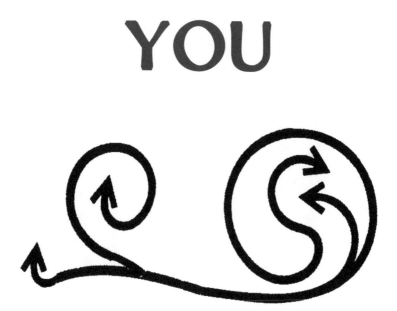

The Leary Library

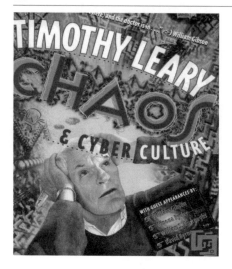

Chaos & Cyber Culture

with
William Gibson,
William
Burroughs,
Winona Ryder
& Others

8.5 x 10.5,   272 pp. $29.95 Hard to get

TIMOTHY LEARY'S "CYBERPUNK MANIFESTO" describes a New Breed that loves technology and uses it to revolutionize communication while having fun creating the cyberdelic politics and culture of the 21st Century. Leary was a leading figure in cyber culture, much as he was a leading figure in the consciousness revolution of the 1960s. *Chaos and Cyber Culture* brings together provocative, futuristic writings and cogent conversations in a graphic format with over 100 illustrations.

> *Leary's humorous, humane, entertaining...romp*
> *through history...I feel my neurons perking up*
> *and snaping to attention...makes the chaos*
> *of our everyday lives sexy.*
> —Susan Sarandon

Politics of Ecstasy

Foreword by Tom Robbins
Introduction by R.U. Sirius
5.5 x 8.5, 232 pp $14.95

EXPLORATION of human consciousness during the "Summer of Love." Social & political ramifications of psychedelic and mystical experience. *Playboy* interview reveals the sexual power of LSD; Leary's classic eight-circuit model of the human nervous system; exploration of Hermann Hesse; effervescent chat with Paul Krassner;impassioned defense of "The Fifth Freedom"— *the right to get high.*

Turn On Tune In Drop Out

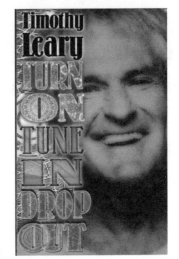

Foreword by Jeffrey Mishlove, Ph.D.
5.5 x 8.5, 162 pp., $14.95

WRITTEN IN THE PSYCHEDELIC 1960s, this is Leary at his best, beckoning with humor and irreverence, visionary of individual empowerment, personal responsibility and spiritual awakening. Includes: Start Your Own Religion • Education as an Addictive Process • Soul Session • Buddha as Drop-Out • Mad Virgin of Psychedelia • God's Secret Agent • Homage to Huxley • The Awe-ful See-er • The Molecular Revolution • MIT is TIM Backwards • Neurological Politics

> *Timothy Leary—in his own inimitable way—has become the twentieth century's grand master of crazy wisdom....*
>
> —Jeffrey Mishlove

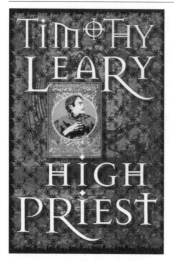

High Priest

Foreword by
Allen Ginsberg

6 x 9, 350 pp. $19.99

Collectors
Limited Edition

Signed by Tim, $100

Numbered, hardcover

16 EARLY PSYCHEDELIC TRIPS lead by

"High priests," including Allen

Ginsberg, Aldous Huxley, Ram Dass, Ralph Metzner, Huston
Smith, and Frank Baron. Each trip has an *I Ching* reading and
marginalia of comments, quotations and illustrations. *Leary is a
hero of American consciousness.* —Allen Ginsburg

Psychedelic
Prayers
& Other
Meditations

with

Ralph Metzner

Rosemary Woodruff Leary

Michael Horowitz

6 x 9, 162 pp. $12.95

MANUAL TO HIGHER CONSCIOUSNESS

inspired by Lao Tse's Tao Te Ching (Way of Life). Poems,
photos and drawings cover of the German edition by H.R.
Giger. Photo of Leary in India

Your Brain Is God

5.375 x 8.375, 112 pp., $11.95

TELLS OF Harvard-Milbrook psychedelic research moving from the scientific to the religious arena after Leary and Alpert came to understand that the US Constitution does not protect scientific exploration. Leary discusses the strong taboo against brain-change.

The brain had replaced the gentials as the forbidden organ that must not be touched or turned on by the owners so the only way in which consciousness-change experiences could be discussed was in terms of philosophic-religious.

—Timothy Leary

Change Your Brain

5.375 x 8.375, 96 pp., $11.95

HOW DRUGS ARE USEFUL TOOLS to reprogram your brain circuits— while having a good time in the process. A compilation of Leary's earliest work at Harvard on "re-imprinting" your brain and the outrage it provoked in stodgy corners of professional and academic psychology. Filled with inside stories and Leary's keen observations of hyprocracy which he reveals with his characteristic humorous cynicism

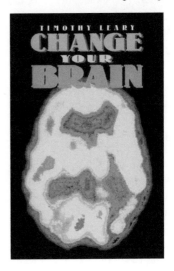

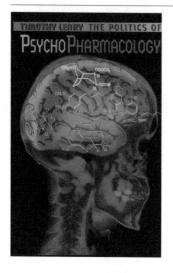

The Politics of Psycho-Pharmocology

with Sasha Shulgin
Rosemary Woodruff Leary
Richard Glen Boire

5.375 x 8.375, 128 pp., $11.95

SAGA OF LEARY'S PERSECUTION. Queen of Hearts-like escape trial. US Senate hearings and interrogation by Teddy Kennedy. Rosemary's account of G. Gordon Liddy in her bedroom. Leary ran for Govenor of California so they threw him in jail. How Tim's lawye smuggled his writing out of prison on the back of Angela Davis fliers. Flamboyant TV interview in Fulson Prison and account of talks with the FBI. Tim was outrageous and we love him for it! If you miss the Sixties, you'll treasure this book.

The Politics of Self-Determination

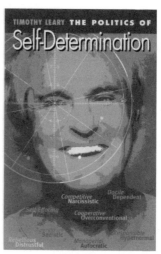

Foreword: Dr. Beverly Potter
5.375 x 8.375, 96 pp.$10.95

AS A GRADUATE STUDENT, Leary created a theory of personality that was a significant catalyst sparking the human growth movement and got him his Harvard appointment— before LSD. Shows Leary's views on personal freedom when he was a young psychologist and how they evolved and morphed by the end of his career. Nestled here and there are glimpses of the ronin attitudes that propelled him and the strategies that he used to get around the system to pursue his research. Leary at his imaginative and provocative best!

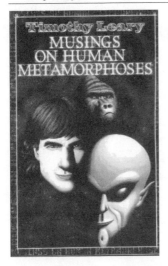

Musings on Human Metamorphosis

5.375 x. 8.375, 128 pp. $11.95

HOW HUMANS ARE MORPHING into space beings—*we are becoming the aliens.* The eight circuits of human metamorphosis, analyzing in depth the consciousness manifested by each. Spinning up the genetic highway, neurogeography of terrestrial politics, and twelve stages of post-cultural evolution. Psychological metamorphosis that precedes the launch of humans into space beings.

Evolutionary Agents

5.5 x 8.5, 192 pp., $12.95

LEARY'S FUTURE HISTORY. Humans and insects comform to hive authority. More on spin. East is past; West is future Pathology proceeds potential. Castes and Alpha Reality. The CIA counter-intelligence makes us stupid. Genetic history andneurogeopraphical determinism. Our terrestrial God is a punk. The Human Race s a race to get smarter. Infilitrate the future! Leary at his imaginative and provocative best..